Warrior of Earth

Kai-Lee Worsley

Happy Birthday, Glynis! ♡

D. Worsley

© Copyright, Kai-Lee Worsley 2022

All rights reserved. This work is protected under the copyright of the Canadian government.

Warrior of Earth
Edited by: Raine Dalrymple, In The Writers Cave
Coverdesign by: Kai-Lee Worsley

To those who dream of a better world, this one is for you.

Contents

1. Time — 8
2. Olympia — 16
3. Messages — 30
4. Betrayal — 53
5. Dimitri — 71
6. Fight or Flight — 93
7. Alone — 105
8. Inner Power — 119
9. Atum — 131
10. Deep Wound — 146
11. Facing Fears — 159
12. The Anova's — 173
13. The Amethyst — 190
14. The Baby — 205

Epilogue: Russia

Prologue

I didn't know what would come next. I only thought of the moment and how agonizing every move felt. Why, was I alive, if I was only here to suffer? Surely God wasn't that out to get me. I thought I had been on good behaviour, my entire life, but suddenly, the things happening around me, started to make cause me to question everything.

I got up again, tired, drained and feeling lost. The only thing I knew at this point, was that I had to continue. I had to fight. There needed to be someone in this world, that did the right thing, no matter how hard it was....and that person...that person was me.

I stood, taller than ever, determination blazing in my deep blue eyes. Fire and ice together. I was born to do the right thing, and so I set off to do it.

1. Time

I have always felt like time was a constant loop, instead of a linear concept, but lately, the days have been seeming to run like years, never coming to an end. Since I've been on my own, running, I have felt everything in life, suddenly seemed to last too long, yet be too short. Where did the time go?

Three months ago, I was living blissfully happy, with everything I have ever wanted. Now here I am, barely knowing what my next move is going to be, and happiness? That is a foreign idea, only visited by me when Dimitri was around to touch my face, and kiss my forehead. Oh, Dimitri....

The name brings sudden pain to my chest and clings to any fibre of my body, willing to feel it. The pain is the only thing I have to motivate me, to keep going, my only hope to in seeing him again.

The sudden urge to vomit pulls me back to reality and I quickly run to the opposite side of the cabin I built. I have never, ever loved vomiting but I guess morning sickness from a baby growing inside of me, is better than a little too many tequilas.

"Oh, son, how I loathe to love you," I say jokingly to keep myself from losing my mind. Who knows if I could find it once it leaves.

Before the love of my life was taken, from me, we had talked about having children. Of course, those conversations went like, "How many should we have?" and "Where should we

raise them?" Now the questions are, "Will my son ever get to meet his father?" and, "Will I ever get to see Dimitri again?"

Sometimes, I close my eyes, and imagine myself with him now and what advice he would give me, "Oh Emilia, your strength is unlike any other, you will get through this and be better because of it."

It brings tears to my eyes to imagine his deep forest green eyes, highlighted with emerald, staring

into my soul and warming me up, like the bare earth. There is so much in his eyes.... love, fierceness, and a will to always defend what is right, no matter what. God, how my heart aches...

I decided, that washing my face with the rain water, I had collected, would snap me back into the real world. It had a wildly fresh feeling, that always helped me feel....

Here, in the corner, where the Pacific Northwest of America, reaches the Pacific North West of Canada, the wilderness is pristine, and a good place to hide in. If they're looking for me, they won't expect me to be right under their nose. Looking in my tiny mirror, I noticed how much older I have gotten. My face, still quite beautiful, had worry written all over it and sleep deprivation, boldly stated, with the dark bags under my deep blue eyes. Thankfully the crystal colour in them helped keep them light.

How was I only twenty-two? Surely, I must be two hundred and two.

With the morning sickness, and the birds chirping, I decided to get to my tasks: fuel my body, the baby, tend to the garden, and find Dimitri. I quickly ran a brush through my long cocoa brown hair and noticed the blonde highlights coming out, from all the time I've been spending outside, in the May spring weather. With While staying off their radar, I've had to make my own shampoo and after the fiftieth attempt, my hair was now smooth and shiny. Like silk hanging from the top of my head to my hips.

Today, I decided to divide it into a top braid from my widows peak to the crown and then two braids, down each side, to all meet in the back, for one big braid. It was the best for gardening and helped keep it strong.

The only clothing I brought with me, were simple outfits. Today felt like a spandex pants and a sweatshirt kind of day. The early mornings were cold here in the middle of nowhere, but not as cold as a fate, possibly waiting for me if I'm caught. The baby hasn't changed my shape much yet, so I haven't had to find anything bigger. I know he's going to be a big boy, and absolutely dread being on the run twenty pounds heavier.

Dawn is my second favourite time of the day, and as I walked out to embrace trees, I was reminded why. The sun sits so beautifully on the horizon, waiting to come and bring us a new day. The earth smells fresh, like water and dirt, with a sprinkle of pine in the air,, that really hits me in my heart. I enjoy time with Mother Earth, as I always have.

Growing up in Alberta, my mother used to bring me hiking, and show me all the herbs I needed to know. I have always been in love with the forest, which explains why I sought refuge in it now.

My mother used to say, "Emilia, now is a perfect time to learn the earth. The way it works, how you can communicate with it, and what it wants to communicate with you. If you respect your mother, she will take care of you, if you do not, then you will be on your own." My mother, Miakoda, is such a wise woman. I wish she were here, with me now.

I know it's better that ~~her she~~ and my father are out of the country, stored away in Greece, where he and Dimitri are both from. ~~there.~~ Luckily, they are safe in the mountain, where they built an off-grid home. My father made me help him and at the time, I was annoyed with all the work, but now that I've had to build my own home, I'm extra thankful to him.

Dimitri's parents live inside the city of Athens, where ~~him~~ he and I met. Unfortunately, in a city that big, I only have to assume that they're being watched, as much as I was. I've been wishing to reach out to anyone but I wouldn't dare. No one needs to be put in danger except me. I'm the one they want.

Deep down I didn't want to be alone, but I knew that I needed to be.

With all of the solitude that has come in the last three-months, I've been able to use my abilities to stay alive, and channel with my guides for help. Working with the earth everyday, I've mastered making plants grow, where I need them to grow, communicating with the sky, to have rain come down, when it's needed, plus having animal companions come by and bring me messages from the outside world.

Apparently, today is one of the days, a message is being delivered because five feet in front of me, a wolf appeared. Wolves are the ones, I feel, the most connected with. Wolves come only when something serious is happening. Usually deer, rabbits, foxes, fox, birds and sometimes even bears come to tell me things. They all bring different messages and meanings but the rare time a wolf comes, means something needs to happen – now.

My deep blue eyes meet his strikingly amber ones. *You need to see this*. He speaks to me through my mind. I know what this means. It means I have to touch the wolf, to be able to see the images in his mind. This happens, through a linking of consciousness, where no bounds boundaries are held.

I gently walked towards him. Even though the animals trust me, I like to remind myself that they are still wild and must be respected. Especially this one, who must be an alpha. His stance is strong and ready for anything, his wise eyes, surveying everything at once. I admire that.

I placed my hand in front, to allow the sniffing of my scent. His gentle air breath against my hand, lets me know, I can continue. Next, is the hard part. In order to connect with the wolf, I have to become very still. I took a deep breath, placed my hand on his head, and began to count. One, two, three breaths and I was in.

Linked with the wolf now, I could see everything he's seen, and could feel everything he's felt. His strongest emotion, was anxiety over other animals, that look like me. It started to make my heart rate quicken. I saw images of the machine's humans bring to the forest and ruins they would leave, the homes of the wolves in.

Seeing all of this, only made me angry, but I was here for a different reason. Pushing that aside I moved further in his mind, calling the message to myself.

It says, run.

It showed me the ones looking for me and that they have grown suspicious. They think I could possibly be in this area, and want to find out. They would be here in twelve hours. I kept watching for more clues and saw an imagine image of Dimitri.

Through the wolfs imagine image of him, I could see worry written all over his handsome features. His brown, loosely curled long hair, was tied tightly in a bun. His deep forest green eyes stared into space and as his hand held his chin up. He stood with his arms crossed over his muscle packed chested, showing just how fit, his body really was. He wore dark jeans and a loose t-shirt, that really accentuated his lofty height. Six-foot-five was high and above average, but then again, so was he.

Maybe he knew I was here and could sense something was wrong. Of course, to the outer world he looked fierce, like a warrior. But I knew those eyes all too well, they're the eyes that speak to my soul.

I took my hand off the wolf, and thanked him for coming.

'Stay safe,' were his last words, before he turned around and headed back into the forest.

Twelve hours, before those monsters arrive... Twelve hours, before Dimitri stands where I stood, now. Quickly realizing I didn't have many options, I decided that leaving the home I had come to love so deeply, was the only one left for me.

Before I left, I had to make sure no one knew it was me here. I gathered all my belongings, which included a backpack with clothes and a blanket. I stuffed the food I had gathered and medical supplies into a duffle bag. One last round to clean up anything, related to a witch like me and the place looked completely different.

Now, it just looked like a creepy abandoned murder shed, but you know what? Better than it actually becoming a murder shed.

But wait.

Dimitri was coming...

The man I have been trying to find, is coming to find me, along with the enemy. Somehow, I needed to send him a message, only he would be able to understand.

I closed my eyes and asked my ancestors to come forward and guide me, in the best way possible. I heard the voice of Elayo, an old soul, from my mother's lineage.

One has to make small signs, only the other half of your heart will understand. What do you have, that only you know?

"Hmmm," I began to pace in front of the cabin. He doesn't know that I'm pregnant, so I can't leave that message. The last night, we spent together, we walked along a trail in a nearby forest, of our home in Portland. Eventually coming to a comfortable, open space. We danced, in the moonlight of the full moon, then he put a *Rosa* behind my ear and asked me to marry him.

Leave the flower behind, and draw the phase of the moon from that night, in the tree bark on the south side of the cabin.

He told me.

"Elayo? Where should I go now?" I asked, confused and at a loss.

You are from the great clan of the warrior's, do you wish to continue to run or do you wish to stand up and defeat your enemy?

The voice of my ancestor was so powerful, just then, I was sure all the birds heard.

I thought about his words. I had always just pictured myself finding Dimitri, sending him a location, and him sneaking away to meet me. I hadn't put much thought into me fighting, because well, I hadn't done much of it in a long time.

Dimitri taught me a lot when we were back in Athens. Always running sprints, or ten kilometres in forty minutes. We would work out and combat train. In return, I helped him open his eyes to his psychic abilities.

I had won a few times, in training sessions with Dimitri, pinning him to the ground after a five-minute sparring session with our hands. Or, even the times when we used wooden swords, to get into the ancient Greek spirit. Those few times, built my confidence because if I could defeat the greatest warrior, I've ever known, then anyone else shouldn't be an issue.

I thought even harder. Dimitri, he is a warrior, and I too. It had to be what I have been running away from. With a big inhale and very loud exhale of breath, I made my decision.

"I want to fight."

2. Olympia

I proceed to do as Elayo suggested and placed a *Rosa*, in a hole of a tree, south of the cabin, and carved a full moon into it. *Rosa*, the wild rose, was one of my favourite flowers. Upon building the cabin, I made sure, to grow as many as possible near by. With my abilities, it was very easy. I just thought of them, placed my hands on the dirt, and spoke a gentle mantra, until I heard the earth tell me, it understood. A week later, I had a flower and then all it took, was getting the seeds out and planting more.

I sighed. All this beauty around me, yet in eleven hours, it would mostly most likely be taken apart and studied like some lab project. Isn't that what humans did anyways? Take things that don't belong to them in the name of "science."

I took one last look at my home, and headed off. The images of what I needed to do were coming to me in visions and I finally knew where to start.

When Dimitri and I were in Athens, he received a call from his aunt. She was the only living relative of his, in the United States, and she wanted him to come and visit. I had an intuitive message that I shouldn't go but tagged along anyways because of my birthplace being was so close. I felt it would be nice, to come back to North America, after ten years.

We arrived to her beautiful home in Portland and instantly fell in love with the land. It held a different feeling than Greece and I wanted to study it more. She opened her home to us and offered for us to move in with her, since she was a new widow, living in a mansion. We kindly accepted and she made all the arrangements herself.

Against my intuition, we began a new life under her roof. All the signs around me screamed for me to leave, but I thought I was just going crazy. After Dimitri was taken, I vanished and never told Sylvia what was going on. Part of me felt awful, leaving the woman who had helped us so much. But the other part, didn't trust anyone around me. Plus, if I was in trouble why would I bring others into it? Now was a different story. I needed to break my own code of ethics and find Sylvia Smith. Off I set.

The trek to civilization was an absolute nightmare. I never knew how tired you could be from being pregnant. I also didn't realize, having to walk from the middle of no where in the Northern part of Washington, to find any other humans, would take so long.

I eventually stumbled into a little town named, Olympia. It didn't look extremely promising, to find a ride, but it was the best thing I'd seen in hours. I found a high school, with a full parking lot and decided to check it out. High school students were nice everywhere, right?

I walked in and looked at the clock. It read back to me, that it was eleven-fourteen in the morning. Wow, it took me eleven hours, to walk here. Eew.

Apparently, this was lunch time for them, because I saw students hurdled in groups. I overheard them talking about the previous hours and lining up to get food from their cafeteria. Some gave me a one over glance, others looked confused and some didn't even notice a stranger, amongst them. I felt a tap on my shoulder and turned around.

"Hi, there!" said a girl with big brown eyes.

She was cute, with short, curly, dark brown hair, half-styled and half who knows. She was tall, which considering, I was being five-foot-ten-inches, was saying a lot. Easily, her lanky body matched my height, which was staggering for someone so young. Her face was innocent and she reminded me of my younger sister, Alexandra. Except she was still alive.

"Hello. Would you be able to direct me to a place where people can get rides to cities?" I asked this cute girl with a kind smile. Surely, she would know. It seemed unlikely that this town, of maybe two thousand, wouldn't have a car-pool option to get better groceries, or anything else.

"Are you from out of town? You look different, but I wouldn't have guessed a big city. You seem like a woods girl. My name is Sophia, but you can call me Sof." She rambled, and I couldn't help but feel my smile getting bigger. So much like Alexandra, I thought wistfully.

"I'm a little bit of both, Sof," no need to tell her I'm basically a walking forest, "but right now, I need to go to Portland." I said, trying to come off, as normal as I possibly could.

The turmoil over my sister's death, always haunted me, and looking at Sophia right now, really tore me apart.

"I love Portland! It's spring break after today, and I have been wanting to visit again. I can drive you after school, if you want! We could get some snacks, and get to know each other. I know this fun game, truth or dare. We play it all the time here. I'm not sure it would be fun in a car but we can try." She sounded excited, and my instants instincts told me, it would be a good idea.

"That's very nice of you Sophia, thank you. My name is Emily, it's great to meet you," I smiled wider, "What time does school end?" I never tell strangers my real name, because when you're a hunted witch, things tend to get a little rocky, when your identity circulates.

I was already very unique looking, at five-foot-ten inches, with an athletic curve to my build. With saying that, my exotic facial features of and high cheekbones, bushy eyebrows, and deep blue eyes with a hint of crystal around the pupils, plus, long, silky cocoa hair to match. There was no telling, that the description with the name Emilia, would only bring trouble.

"It's over at two-forty. After that, we can go home to my mom and ask her if it's okay. She's pretty chill but will want to meet you." said Sophia.

"Of course, I'll be back to meet you here, at two-forty this afternoon. Sophia, is there anywhere I can hangout until then? Maybe a restaurant?" I asked, realizing I was starving.

"There is a local diner on second street, just northeast about three blocks from here. Their salads are really good, but I go for the milkshakes, chocolate is my favourite," she said smiling even wider. I wasn't sure a human face could be so bright and full of light, but she proved me wrong. I smiled, and we said our goodbyes.

I headed off to the diner. I hadn't eaten in a public place in a long time and I had to admit, I was nervous. Sophia had been my first interaction, that wasn't with an animal or a spirit in over three months. She was pleasant but I knew most humans, were not that happy.

I took a deep breath, closed my eyes and tilted my head up to the sky. I heard an eagle swoop down and land on a tree branch near by. "Hey old friend, what brings you here?" I asked.

Remember to watch everything at once, reality may not be as it seems. His eyes spoke to me, showing just how strong of a spirit he was.

Take this for protection. Then a feather dropped onto the ground, and he flew away.

I picked the feather up and put it away immediately. I then wondered which part of my reality he was referring to. It all seemed brutally harsh to be a lie.

I arrived at the diner, that was in fact, very close to the school. A big sign hung in front, advertising their milkshakes.

"She wasn't kidding." I chuckled recalling Sophia's words.

I hoped something that said FAMILY OPERATED DINER, meant that it would be good. I was about to face a lot of fears, and this apparently was the first hurdle.

I sat down in a booth facing the door, and put my belongings opposite of me. I never liked having my back exposed, so I picked a spot in the corner. There were indeed, some high school students hurrying to get back, running out the door, with some to-go containers.

My eyes swept over some older locals sitting together, playing chess. There were two tables, with games going on and I wondered if there was a king's court thing set up.

A fairly large woman walked up to my table, in some high heels, that I could feel were hurting her. Instantly, I felt where the pain was in her body and where the energy was clogged inside her muscles. I knew she was tired of working at this diner and wanted to be anywhere but here.

"Hi there, what can I get started for you?" she said, automatically like a robot.

"Hello," I said, politely, "I will start with a water and a chamomile tea please."

"Sorry sweetheart, no chamomile tea here. Only green, and peppermint. Either of those interest you?" She said, almost apologetic – almost.

"Peppermint, please." I smiled and she walked away. I looked down at the menu to see what could be good. I was the hungriest I've ever been.

While I lived in the forest, I had to hunt and grow my own food. I didn't hunt a lot, but with the baby growing, I felt weaker if I didn't eat enough. When I decided I had to hunt, I asked Mother Earth for help. She gave me the help I needed, and always provided for me. In return, I used every part of the animal, so that their sacrifice was worthy.

Nothing at this diner, came even close to that. I skimmed through the sections and saw that they had no theme to the food, just whatever they could make. I came across a pasta recipe, that couldn't hurt too much.

"Did you decide on what to eat?" The waitress, Bethany on her name tag, said when she placed my water and tea down. I felt her pain again and had the urge to do something. I subtly sent her light energy, and envisioned strength from the earth, coming through me to her, like a clear crystal middle woman, doing the work of Spirit. I felt her ease up a bit and when she looked at me to take my order, a little of her dark mood vanished.

This was something I knew how to do, from all of the time spent with my mother growing up. She taught me that I could heal everything, including humans. Usually, they needed to give me permission. Maybe she was open to the help subconsciously and that's why it worked.

"I'll take the basil pasta dish, no cheese please." Trying to eat dairy after so long, could only mean trouble for my body. I didn't like it much anyways, but every once in a while, I would have some with wine in Greece.

Bethany nodded, "Garlic bread on the side?" she asked.

"Sure," I nodded.

Bethany took my menu and promised the food quickly. I decided to look around the diner some more, opening myself, to those around me, carefully. I didn't need a tidal wave of emotion and energy knocking me down, but I wanted to get a feel – literally, and figuratively – of this town.

Everyone's spirit was a little sad, like a tragic event had happened recently. I couldn't feel individuals, but I could feel the overall human spirit, in the place I was. It was easier for me to link with animals than it was humans.

"You must be cheating!" One of the older gentleman exclaimed, from one of the chess tables.

"You're just upset that you aren't the king of chess," said another gentleman. His voice was low, and carried tons of charisma. He reminded me of Morgan Freeman, they could've been twins. This guy had wise brown eyes, with early signs of glaucoma, but I had a feeling he didn't need his eyes to see. His hair was short and a mix of black and white. The skin he had showed barley showing, barely had any signs of aging. The only way I could figure out his age was by his hands. They had veins sticking up on the skin, wrapped in a thin nut-brown coating.

"There is no way you can beat everyone all the time. We all play everyday, we're good too!" said the accuser. I didn't need any magical powers, to know this guy was about to blow like a volcano. I wanted to look in his eyes, to see what could be causing, such an emotional outburst.

I spoke too soon. The man looked up and caught my eyes. I froze, feeling weird at the timing. "Are you new?" He asked with a snark in his tone.

"Just passing through, sir." I replied flatly. No need to specify or get too friendly. I wanted to leave this town with little memory of me.

The Morgan Freeman doppelgänger turned around to look me over. There was something in his eyes that caught my attention. I wasn't able to link with human's individual consciousness, but their eyes betrayed enough sometimes, for me to get the information I wanted.

"Where are you coming from, young lady?" Morgan asked in a kind, curious tone.

"I'm travelling down from Victoria, BC." Small lie, but "I was in the middle of the woods about eighty miles north of here," doesn't really sound that very sane.

"Canada is a beautiful place. My niece is in Vancouver, she's in some television show that they film up there." Morgan said to me, with a small smile, clearly proud of his niece.

"Oh, how nice" I replied with my own.... trying to get a deeper look into his eyes.

The other man, who looked more like Woody Harrelson, but thirty years older said, "Here we go again, bragging about your niece. Can we get back to the game?" he snarled.

"Nice talking to you, if you have any questions, please ask." Morgan said. It was a normal comment but delivered with a look that said, he knew exactly what I was trying to do.

I panicked. If he figured that out, what else did he know? Who sent him here? Was I in danger? My head started spinning, just as Bethany came to deliver the pasta.

"Here you go sweetheart, no cheese. God knows you could use the extra pounds."

I nodded, and she left. If I wasn't having an anxiety attack. I would've rolled my eyes at that comment, but no time for sarcasm when your heart beats dangerously high. Heart attacks at twenty-two were rare, right?

I took a big sip of water, telling myself that I was safe, and had everything I needed, in case I had to flee. I drank the entire glass, then noticed how thirsty I really was.

"Bethany," I spoke loud enough for her to hear. She was close by, chatting with Morgan and Woody.

She turned to me, "Yes?"

"Would you be able to get me some more water, please?" I asked holding the glass up.

"Sure thing, sweetheart," she said as she approached and took the glass to the kitchen.

I turned to grab my fork, and dug into the pasta. I was so hungry that before Bethany got back, I was almost done my food.

"You sure can eat for a tiny thing like yourself," she commented as she put the water down.

I swallowed, "Yeah I'm pretty hungry, can I order some fries too?"

"Sure thing, coming right up." said Bethany.

I hesitantly glanced at the chess table, before getting back to my food. Morgan looked at me and spoke.

Come play a round after you've finished.

I was startled. Completely wide-eyed. I probably looked like I saw a ghost. I nodded slightly, and turned back to the food. Fuel the body, feed the baby, was my new mantra. If this child was going to be half me and half Dimitri, he would need all the nutrition he could get.

I finished as Bethany brought the fries with some ketchup. She placed them down and I practically inhaled them too, ignoring how hot and fresh they were.

After finishing the fries, water and tea, I looked up to see the bench opposite of Morgan, empty. Every other chess player was at the first table, watching the match. I placed all the dishes together neatly and left money for the bill on the table. Before fleeing Portland, I took out a hefty amount of cash, so I always had a lot on me.

I took a deep breath and reminded myself that I was a warrior, capable of handling a conversation in a diner with a stranger.

I grabbed my belongings and walked over to the king of chess.

"No need for formalities I supposed," I said, as I slid into the bench placing my stuff beside me, close to the window. "My name is Myles. Close to Morgan, but not quite." He smirked.

"You were listening to my thoughts!" I whispered in a harsh tone. How dare he?

"You were trying to listen to mine. I thought it was only fair. Besides, you were feeling out the entire place and I was curious as to what you would find. I don't have that ability and wanted to see how it worked. Would you like to play?" His hand motioned over the chess bored.

He spoke so casually that it irritated me. How could he not understand, this was an important topic to be quiet about!

"No." I said firmly. His attitude was annoying me, but I was kinda curious, to see what he could do.

"I'll tell you what, young lady. If you can beat me, then I'll tell you what you want to know, and if I beat you, then you tell me the truth about Victoria, BC." He winked.

"You haven't already searched my memory to find out?" I rolled my eyes. Like this guy didn't already know. If he knew I kept calling him Morgan, he obviously knew more.

"No, I can only hear what you think about in the present. Not what you have thought in the past," he leaned closer to me and whispered, "Thats why I am always sitting on this bench when we play." He smiled and gestured around, like it truly was his kingdom.

You know what, if I was about to take down an army, I could take down this old man. What was chess, besides war on a board?

"Alright, let's play," I said.

I had only played chess a few times. Every time it was with Dimitri, and he beat me, almost always.

"Come on! Why do you always beat me in everything!?" I exclaimed at him one day after the fifth match. "Because, Emilia, you are not focused. You watch me more than you watch the board. Pay attention to all the details, and think three steps ahead. That is how you can outsmart the enemy," he said to me in a diplomatic way. "You're so annoying," I replied as I rolled my eyes. "Yet, you stick around," he said smiling with his beautiful full smile. The one that always made my heart melt and think it was unfair, to be such a perfect human being. "Alright big shot, let's go again and I'll watch the board." I said as I lined up all my pieces. That day it took me nine rounds just to win one. Thinking about it now, brought that same pain it always did, to my chest when I thought about him. He was always so patient and kind. Leading when needed but knowing when to take a moment and teach those around him. He was truly a perfect human. "You going to go, or make me wait till I turn ninety-seven?" asked Myles, bringing me back to our present chess match.

 I looked away from the chess board, up at him, then back down again. I played several scenarios in my head, but knew if I could make a few more moves I would have him. I felt a tickle in my mind and knew it was Myles sticking his nose – figuratively – where it didn't belong.

I shot him a warning look, then wrapped myself in light, mentally putting up a barricade around my mind. It was a technique my mother had taught me to keep away bad dreams. I figured the principle was the same here and by the look of his shocked face, it worked. His eyes seemed to say that was a new thing to him, and I smiled at the victory. Checkmate grandpa.

 I made my move, which was followed by his, then I retaliated, advancing my plan. The next move he made was a very smart one and then came, "checkmate young lady."

 "What!" I exclaimed, no way had I let this match slip. "Yup. Read-em and weep," he said with his hands sweeping the board. "I am the king of the court, once again" he sat back, smiling a full smile revealing a gold tooth on the left side of his mouth.

"Ugh," was the only thing I could manage besides a rant of swear words, that would for sure turn some heads and gain attention.

I closed my eyes and opened them, "Alright, what do you want to know?"

A brief look of surprise flashed in his eyes, like he almost couldn't believe I was being true to my word. Something I would've taken offence to, but I was too baffled I lost to even care.

"Well, let's start with why are you here?" began Myles.
"To eat. Why else would I come to a diner?" He was going to have to be a little more specific, if he wanted to drag me through the dirt.

"Sore loser." He shrugged. "You know I meant, 'why are you in this town?' Let's start with that."

"I'm here because I stumbled upon it and thought it would be a good place to find a ride to a city." I met his scrutinizing eyes unflinching. Myles might be somewhat like me, but I wasn't going to get in bed, with someone I didn't know. The less information the better.

"What do the Anova's want from you?" Myles asked, straight faced.

My heart panicked at the word but I tried to hide the shock of the question. The Anova's were the group I'd been alluding this entire time. The one's that took my love, Dimitri and robbed me of his touch. The one's I've feared, and the one's I was planning to take down.

I wondered how he knew about that. No time to ask now, so I stored that question for later.

"I'm not quite sure yet, but I'm going to find out." I said firmly.

"Well, all I's know is it can't be anything good," he took out a pen and started writing on a napkin, then handed me it, "here, keep this. Think of it as a 'get out of jail free card," he said seriously.

"Thank you. I have to go and meet someone now, but I will keep this with me," I said as I started to get up. Myles grabbed my hand and looked me dead in the eyes, making my standing up look a little sloppy, as I fumbled. "Be careful. Keep things to yourself and remember to have your own back. There are many people that wish to get their hands on someone like you and especially on the child inside of you. There's a powerful spirit in both of you, that will be disruptive to many people. Sophia Johnson is a great girl, with a nice family. You can trust her, but that's it. Well, and me, but that will be for you to decide." He spoke in a low voice, never moving his hand. The only response I gave was a nod, then I headed off.

3. Messages

Before leaving the diner, I got Sophia a chocolate milkshake, figuring it would break the ice a little more, since it was her favourite. I hurried back to the school. The sooner I got to Sylvia's house, the better.

"Hey! Oh, is that for me?!" Sophia exclaimed as she ran over to me and took the shake, "thank you, thank you, thank you. Just what I need after that chemistry class. Man, that subject is hard."

I started to smile, I loved anything to do with chemistry, math, biology, art, english, literature. Basically, anything with books, it had EMILIA LOVES written all over it. "Glad I could help, let's rock."

She explained, it was only a five-block walk and that she only took the car when it was chilly. Because it was such a beautiful day, she decided to walk. I wished it was a rainy day, my legs were aching.

We got to her house just in time for her to finish the milkshake. She hadn't said a word the entire time. I hope no one would ever introduce her to alcohol, with the way she clung to this milkshake.

"That was great, thank you again," she said, beaming with even more happiness than when I met her a few hours ago.

"You're welcome," I replied with a small smile as we entered her home.

It was a nice place. A modern style home, with new furniture. The colour palette of navy, cream, and grey, made it look, as if it was supposed to be, on Architecture Digest.

It looked like one of the nicest houses on the block, meaning, her family was probably wealthy in some way. I could've guessed that by her clean, designer clothing and school bag but I didn't want to judge too quickly.

"Hi Sof! We're in the kitchen," said a fairy like female voice.

"Hi mom, I brought a friend home from school. Since it's spring break, we're thinking of going to Portland," Sophia gestured to me, "Mom this is Emily, Emily, my mom, Victoria. Aunt Elizabeth this is Emily, Emily, Aunt Elizabeth."

I held my hand out to shake, "Hello Ma'am, this is a lovely home you have," I said to Victoria, then turned to Elizabeth, "Hello, I love your blouse. Where did you get it?"

They exchanged looks like I was some sort of alien child, but that's fine. I was.

"Thank you, you can call me Victoria."

"And me Elizabeth. As for the blouse, I got it at a thrift shop in Seattle. They always have such pleasant things," Elizabeth said. Her voice wasn't as fairy like, but rather held the tone of someone more aloof.

"So, mom, can we go?" asked Sophia with a pouty face that would be hard to say no to.

"Sure, but your aunt and I were thinking of going to Portland, as well. Maybe we can all go together? Like a fun road trip!" Victoria suggested, in such an excited attitude, that I almost felt bad about having to ditch them for my own plan.

"That sounds like fun," I automatically said, before Sophia could protest. Years of training in my family, had taught me that when someone was willing to help you out, you couldn't be too picky with what you got.

"Great!" Elizabeth and Victoria said in unison. "I'll go pack, come on Emily, you can see my room." Sophia gestured as we walked down the hallway and up the stairs. Once we got to her room, I was so happy to see a bed that I plopped on it like it was the righteous cloud I had been searching for all day.

"I hope you don't mind, that my mom and aunt want to come? I'm sorry about that, they get excited about travel. Sometimes, I wish I could just go do things alone, without parental supervision all the time." Sophia began, "I almost feel like they don't trust me to go out. I know, since Gary went missing, things have been weird but its not like I can't handle myself," she said.

I thought about that for a moment. I was a complete stranger, and they welcomed me in, like they knew me for years. It was probably in their best interest that they were protective. If anything, they should've questioned me more.

"Who's Gary?" I asked, staring up at the ceiling. Maybe this was why the energy at the diner was so low. Had I struck gold in finding one person, out of two thousand that knew?

"He's the owner of the diner. He went missing about two-months ago and no one has seen him since. It shocked a lot of the people in the town," she explained.

"Do you know why anyone would want to take him?" I was curious to see if this had anything to do with the Anova's.

"He was kind of a jerk. He picked on one of the senior's there a lot named Myles. Gary kind of had, like a mean energy to him, like a dark cloud was always following him." I heard her moving things around, in her room but didn't bother to look.

"Huh, that's interesting," I replied, no longer mentally in the room. I pondered… Myles didn't seem sad like everyone else. He was happy to continue playing chess at his rivals diner, even though Gary had been missing for a while.

Bethany, the waitress, didn't want to be there anymore. The Woody Harrelson guy must've been the most effected because he was so irritable.

Sophia said it seemed like a dark cloud followed Gary around… Something about this was weird, but didn't take priority with in my life right now.

Victoria came upstairs and asked if we would be okay, driving to Portland tomorrow, then offered me to stay the night, at their house.

"Why do you have so many things with you?" she asked before leaving the room.

"Oh, I have an aunt that lives there and wanted to bring her some of her favourite things." I sat up, slightly lying. Sylvia was technically my aunt-in-almost-law. Dimitri was my fiancè, so I might as well skip the wedding and claim him as my husband. I'm sure he wouldn't mind missing the imaginary ceremony.

32

"That's very thoughtful of you, dinner will be ready by six-thirty if you girls want to go out and do something. Just be back by then, I'm making home-made pizzas." Victoria's voice carried toward us, as she walked out.

I looked at the clock. Three-forty-five. I turned over to Sophia.

"Sof, would it be okay if I took a nap? I've been outside a lot and kind of just want to stay in," I asked, trying to mimic her puppy face, most likely failing the cute innocent look she could pull off.

"Yeah, totally fine with me! I have a lot of homework to do, I'll start, so we can enjoy Portland, some more." she told me earnestly, like she truly believed we were all going to have a great, girls trip. I thought I made it clear, when I asked a random high schooler for a ride that I just needed a ride? Things were certainly weird in this town.

I got into my make shift bed on the floor and fell asleep, as soon as I hit the pillow. During my sleep I heard a few voices, "Emily?" "Emily, hi?" But they eventually went away and let me slumber.

I woke up, just in time to see dawn, my favourite time. I looked down at myself, still in my clothes from the previous day. Someone must have added another blanket to my bed because I had more bedding, than just my one blanket, from the cabin.

A quick glance around the room, showed me that I was indeed inside someone's home and then I remembered yesterday. Sophia, Victoria, Elizabeth, and Myles. I sure wasn't in the woods any more.

I got up to use the bathroom and stumbled around, trying to find it, in the dark home. Eventually finding it, I felt the wall until I got to the switch, flicking on the light.

"What a luxury," I mumbled to myself. I didn't have power or running water in the cabin. It made me a lot more creative, in ways, that I did 'everyday' things. Being around it again was something I was going to have to readjust to.

After I finished, I stopped to look at myself in the mirror. Wow, I looked rough. Almost like someone had come and punched me in the face, but left no bruises. I looked exhausted and in need of a makeover.

I washed my face and brushed my hair, then put it in a neat, French, braid, to keep it from getting all 'mad scientist' again. I stumbled back to Sophia's room, and looked out the window.

"Caw, Caw" a crow landed on the window's ledge. I looked at it and asked it to come back later, when I could touch it. The messages came clearer when I could feel the animal.

However, I learned that if their spirit was strong enough, I could make eye contact and hear it. Sadly, more often than not, I needed to feel the being, to connect with their consciousness.

The crow seemed to understand because he tilted his head slightly, then flew away. I stared out the window for a few more minutes and then decided it would be okay for me to get more rest. I would need it, and there were no crops to be taken care of. Just me and the baby.

I was woken up later, to a rustling of blankets, and sudden tiptoeing around my bed, to get out the door. I peaked over the blankets and saw Sophia, trying extremely hard not to wake me.

"Morning Sof," I said cheerfully, making her practically leap in the air. I chuckled when she did.

"Oh, my goodness," she said with a hand over her heart, "I didn't mean to wake you, I just have to use the bathroom."

"No worries, I was already awake. Hey, sorry for missing dinner last night. I was so tired, I guess I just needed rest." I felt genuinely bad for missing it but happy I got to sleep so much.

"It's okay, my mom wasn't upset or anything but she was confused, as to why you were so tired. We tried really hard to wake you up, and all you kept saying was, 'send the message later,' I think she'll ask you about it. I told her, you are a friend of a girl at my school and we met that way. So, if

she asks, you've known Brianna for years. She's new here so my mom doesn't know their family well enough, to ask more questions," She said quietly and quickly.

"Okay great, thank you."

"But, Emily? Why are you here and are you okay?" I was proud that someone in this world finally asked me a serious question.

"Yeah, I'm just... uh.. dealing with a lot of stuff right now and haven't been able to rest like that, in a while. I'm okay today and that's what matters. I've been having, as some would say, bad days recently, but I prefer to think of them as character building days," I said in a mouth full, surprised at my own willingness, to offer up so much insider information.

I didn't feel comfortable with a lot of people like I do with nature. You know, natures intentions, hunt, stay alive, protect their own. When they let their guard down, they do it because they feel comfortable around you, sometimes to offer, to receive love. Pure intentions.

Humans are wild cards. You never know what they're planning behind their eyes. But, sometimes, if you know what to look for, their true being is easier to spot. I could see in Sophia's eyes, that she was very kind hearted and trustworthy. There were only a few people in my life, I saw those qualities in and none were around right now, except her. I guess I just had to go with the flow on this one.

"Do you like, need any help?" she asked, giving me a look that told me she meant it.

"Well yeah, the ride to Portland." I chuckled.

"Oh, right, yeah duh. I'll be right back, I still have to use the bathroom," she said, leaving the room quietly. I got up and started to fold my blankets when I heard a soft knock on the door.

"Hi, Emily? Can I come in?" said a familiar fairy voice.

"Oh yes, Victoria. Come in," I said turning towards the door to face her. "I'm sorry about missing dinner last night, I was really tired from walking a lot yesterday, that I just needed to rest," I began.

She held up her hand, "No need to apologize. I'm actually here to ask you something else."

"Sure, what's up?"

"Have you met Myles Richard?" asked Victoria, eyeing me suspiciously.

"Yes, I actually lost to him, in chess, yesterday," I said, rolling my eyes at the memory.

"Ah, king of the court," she smiled, "anyways, he called yesterday, to ask if you were here. I asked why he was interested and he just said to pass along a message," she said, as she handed me a folded piece of paper.

"Oh, weird..." I said as I took it. What could he be saying to me? And why?

"He is a nice man. He also mentioned, that you're somewhat of a nomad and that it was your first time in town. Sophia said you were friends with some new people, but I have the feeling she may be telling me a small lie. Now, I'm not upset. She's a great person and you seem kind as well, but if I'm going to take you both somewhere and also make you breakfast, I need to know the truth. Now." She said firmly.

As she spoke, I took in more of her features. She looked like a tiny fairy, I realized. She must've only been about five foot-five-inches but with that fierce tone, we seemed to be the same height. She had shoulder length light brown hair, curly like Sophia's, but more tamed and a noticeable difference of eyes, that looked jade, instead of Sophia's deep brown ones.

The truth hey? Alright...

"Well, I'm coming from the northern part of Washington. I was there, on a retreat, to connect with nature. I had to come back into town to get a ride, so that I could make it to Portland. I need to see my aunt because I believe she may be able to help me with a problem I'm dealing with. I actually met Sophia yesterday, because I thought a high schooler would be able to point me in the right direction for a carpool, but she offered herself," I began. "I also didn't get the chance to offer her money, which I can now. I didn't expect to stay the night either but I would be more than happy to give you money for that, as well," I said, putting my hands over my uterus. I guess holding my unborn child was a new comfort mechanism. I also wanted to keep down the vomiting feeling, I was starting to get.

She looked me up and down and stared into my eyes, just as Sophia walked into the room.

"Good morning, Sof," said Victoria, never taking her eyes off of me. Apparently either sizing me up to take me down, or seeing if I was lying or not, which honestly, I wasn't, really…

"Everything okay in here?" asked Sophia, clearly reading the room.

Victoria finally broke her gaze on me, and directed all that attitude right at her daughter. "You have your heart in the right place Sophia but you are not allowed to lie to me. The next time you lie, I will not be so kind, in letting your new friend stay at our home, or allowing you the freedom of a road trip. Do I make myself clear?" She firmly stated, as she looked at Sophia, with that same scrutinizing look, she was just giving me.

"Yes, mom. I'm sorry. I just had a good feeling about Emily, and really, really wanted to go to Portland." Sophia said, pleading her case.

"I understand," she said, turning to me, "well then, I guess we'd better get going, so we can get you back to your aunt, to solve your issue."

"Thank you." I said, smiling.

"Breakfast in ten, then we leave in thirty." said Victoria as she left.

38

"I'm sorry," Sophia and I both said to each other automatically, once her mom left the room.

Then we both burst into laughter. She really did remind me of Alexandra and it made me both sad and happy at the same time. Maybe I didn't completely lose a sister, after all.

"I didn't mean to sell you out. She just gave me a look and I couldn't lie to her." I said, apologetically, shaking my hands, to emphasize the pressure I felt.

"Its okay, she can be scary. You wouldn't think so because she's so short, but don't let that fool you. I may be five-foot-nine-inches but compared to her I'm like an ant." Sophia said smiling.

We finished cleaning up, then went down for breakfast. There on the counter, I saw the most beautiful thing in the world. Waffles.

Not just any kind, but the extremely fluffy and good kind. And did they ever smell delicious. I could feel my saliva getting ready to indulge in the fluffy goodness. I almost ate enough for four people and only stopped myself when I could barley move.

After breakfast, we headed upstairs, to finish packing and then back down to the car. Elizabeth pulled in, just then.

"Hi ladies! Are we ready for a great day?" She exclaimed. Her attitude was different today and felt a little inauthentic. "We sure are," Victoria spoke, as she packed the stuff in the trunk of Elizabeth's Porsche SUV.

I climbed in the backseat, with Sophia, and sat behind the passenger seat, giving me time to study Elizabeth's features a little more.

She had straight blonde hair, with brown roots coming out at the top. Jade green eyes as well, but not as much soul behind them, as her sister's and definitely not as much soul behind them, as her niece's. Her eyebrows were done nicely, and her nails were freshly manicured. She wore designer sunglasses, and tight clothing. Different from Victoria who wore nice clothing but seemed to keep it comfortable and less flashy.

Victoria got in the car, and just as we were about to pull out, I heard the crow again, reminding me of earlier this morning. It sounded urgent, so it must've meant something important needed to be shared.

"Oh, I uh, have to step out really quickly. I feel a little nauseous." I said, as I opened the door. It wasn't a lie. I did feel nauseous.

"Do you need anything?" asked Elizabeth.

"No, that's fine, just two minutes of fresh air should work." I said closing the door and turning my attention to the crow. I walked closer and knelt down, so I could hide the fact that I was about to pet a wild animal. They knew I was weird, but how weird did I want to appear?

I touched the crow, and was instantly pulled to the urgent matter. The Anova's had found the camp and were searching everything for clues, that it was me. I heard a lot of, "it could've been," "but would she have survived?" "she's a witch! she's unnatural, she can probably hear us right now." That last one was funny 'cause I could, indeed, hear them. Then it flashed to Dimitri... Oh, my... Dimitri... He went around south to look for tracks and stumbled upon the *Rosa* flower I had been instructed to put in the tree with the full moon carving. He twisted it around his finger, and then smelled the flower.

"My love," he spoke softly, "how I miss you so. It was you here. I can feel you. I miss you. If you can hear this, know that I love you, more than life itself." He then put the flower inside his jacket pocket and traced the full moon with his finger tips.

Then the scene went back to the leaders of the party. One of them looked so familiar but I couldn't place him. He spoke, "can we trust him? Do you think he knows? If he does then he has to go. We can't risk exposing SSA to anyone."

Another man replied "I don't think he knows, he's just here because he knows the girl well enough. We bait her with him, then once we have her, we dispose of him."

I took my hand off of the crow, and was truly nauseous now. He blinked a few times, then flew away. Dispose of him? SSA? Bait me? What in the world was going on here. And who was that guy I recognized? Was Dimitri learning his abilities and could he feel me, if I was close? How close could I be? How strong was he? Could I take down these guys down and get my family back?

"Emily, are you okay?" I heard Sophia from the car. Right, present problems. I needed to mull all this over and an hour car ride further away from them, was probably the best thing for me, right now.

I got up and went back into the car.

"Yeah, thank you for waiting, that helped a lot." Really, it only made things worse, I guess today, was another character-building day in the life of Emilia Diomades.

We started to drive up and down hills, through winding roads into the sun, then into rain. The scenes passing by me were stunning. Everywhere I looked there was green,

green, and more green. Trees were blooming from all the rain and you could see how beautiful spring really was. Life coming back in full swing from a season of rest, it felt like the most beautiful thing in the world and I shed a few tears.

"What's wrong?" Sophia asked leaning in.

"It's just so beautiful," I replied, still amazed at the moment unfolding around me.

I watched it, until the rain became so heavy, it put my mind at ease and I allowed myself a moment to process. The Anova's found my camp, but weren't sure it was me that was there. They're using Dimitri to lure me, but why me? And why was Dimitri with them anyways? When he disappeared, Sylvia had told me it was to do with a secret government mission. Better yet, who are the Anova's really? The only things thing I knew for sure, were was what they were capable of.

I thought back to my life before this whole mess. Since I could remember, I've always been able to see things, I couldn't explain or know things prior to them happening. What really changed me, was after my sister, Alexandra, died. No one to this day, has found her murderer and it pushed me to into deep solitude.

One day, Alexandra and I were in the woods, in our home town Hinton. It was just before my twelfth birthday, and it was a chilly fall day. We were picking the last of the wild blueberries and laughing about things our mom used to tell us, Alexandra was older than I, by a year, making her thirteen at the time.

"Do you remember that one day she told us, if we kept lying, our noses would grow and grow and never stop?" Alexandra said referring to our mother, Miakoda Diomades.

"Yes! It scared me so badly I made a promise to myself that I would never lie again." I laughed in response. "Do you ever think about what it would be like to fly, Emilia?" she asked, suddenly changing the topic. "I think about it, all the time," I said as we both looked up to a raven landing on a tree branch beside us. The raven looked at us and then Alexandra held out her hand that held blueberries in it. The raven looked, and then ate some.

"What is it like to fly for you, Raven?" she asked. To my upmost utmost surprise, I heard a new voice in my head that spoke, *It feels like magic. I truly feel the work of spirit every time I take flight.*

"Wha... just happened? Did you hear that!? He answered! He heard you! He knew!" I exclaimed, in total shock. I thought I was going insane. Surely, I couldn't have heard the voice of a raven.

"Remember when mom said we are all connected beings and that our ancestors could feel spirit through everything?" she said as she stroked the feathers of the raven gently. "Well, she was right. We can feel it, Emilia. We are chosen to do great things, be great warriors of Earth. All you have to do, is feel the power inside of you and let it be known. Let it be seen. We have a gift. *You* have a gift. We must accept what we have and use it for good."

I was so stunned, that I couldn't even think of a response at the time. The raven flew off and we headed back home for dinner.

"Hello, my beauties. Welcome back. How was the picking?" My mother asked upon our return.

"Fine," I said, hoping my nose wouldn't grow. "It was great, mom, I think Emilia learned a lot." "Ah, yes, Emilia the scholar and Alexandra the teacher.

You two make a perfect pair." she said smiling. "Where's dad?" I asked.

"He's out getting some water from the well. Alexandra, set the table," my mother said. That was the last night we all ate together as a family.

A sudden question brought me back to the present. "We're almost there, Emily. What would you like to do? We rented a nice place, with four bedrooms, three bathrooms, a pool, a hot tub, and an indoor theatre. You're welcome to stay with us for a few days. Or we can take you to your aunt. It's up to you."

I thought about this and didn't want to appear ungrateful, for everything these strangers had done for me. They took me in and cared for me. How could I turn them down?

"That sounds like a lot of fun, I would like to join you and contribute in whatever way I can," I said, at last.

"This is going to be awesome!" Sophia was beaming with excitement. You would think we had been friends for years, with how happy she seemed to be, spending even more time with me.

As I looked at her, I realized I was excited to spend some more time with her as well. I decided I would stay with them but also work the case. I could sneak to Sylvia's house, to see her periodically.

It could work and that was my decision. I told myself to allow it and release the guilt and tension I was feeling. It was somewhat effective.

We reached the rented house and it indeed was just as gorgeous, as I had imagined. It was located, just outside of downtown Portland and was close enough to see the views of the mountains, showing a contrast of urban and rural life.

The house had a brick exterior, with marble pillars and bushes covering the yard, to create privacy. There were beautiful french windows, that were open wide, giving it an inviting feel. We walked inside, to see marble flooring in the foyer, with a big elaborate staircase, up on the left side. Burgundy covered walls contrasted the whiteness of the floor and gold decorations were placed as accents. It looked like a castle from the ancient days, with hits of modern taste. It felt more like home than Silvia's house, where Dimitri and I had lived nine months ago.

"This is a good pick, V, great job," Elizabeth said, praising her sister while looking around, wide-eyed. "Thanks Lizzie, I decided we could all use a fun, stress free vacation," replied Victoria, clearly satisfied with her pick.

"Mom, what are we going to eat? I'm starving. Can we order pizza and eat in the pool?" asked Sophia. Eat in the pool? Is that what teenagers wanted to do these days?

"Yes, we can. Why not? How about some ice cream with that too?"

"Yes please!" Elizabeth, Sophia and I all said in unison. Victoria and Elizabeth headed out in the car to get some junk food, leaving Sophia and I to explore the house.

We walked up the gorgeous marble staircase to our assigned bedrooms. I went off into mine to check it out and change my clothes.

As I went in and looked around the room, I saw just how much work, must've went into building this house. My room was filled with the same ancient modern twists as the foyer. I had a gorgeous queen-sized bed, covered with a beautiful chrism red blanket and accented with a white satin sheet set.

I couldn't help but think that adding a lot of plants would've given this room a nice touch. I had my own bathroom, that too was marble with gold accents. The towels hanging, were white, and the shower was incredibly beautiful. It was a walk-in shower, with stone and a couple side jets, ready to wash you like a car. It included a chair inside, a sauna option, and a built-in stereo.

'Talk about opulence," I said to myself as I studied it more. Such luxuries were welcomed into my life, even though I also liked living simply in the forest.

I decided, now would be a good time for a shower and grabbed a fresh set of clothing. Since I didn't have much, there was only one nightgown, two sweaters, a hoodie, two pairs of sweats, four

t-shirts, a pair of spandex shorts, spandex pants and one pair of jeans, which I was already wearing. Deciding to go for the spandex shorts and t-shirt combo, I brought that along with some fresh underwear back to the bathroom. I started to take off my clothes off, and the note Victoria gave me fell out. I nearly had forgotten about that. I picked it up, and opened it.

I write in urgency. The A-Team is in town, and stopped by the diner. I spoke with a very tall man, he sees us. Find him, he is in danger. Remember what I told you,
M.

Decoding was not a strength of mine, but I could guess what Myles was trying to say. The Anova's had found the town and stopped by the diner. Which is surprising because I purposely covered my tracks and that town is in the middle of literally, no where. I wonder how they did that? A very tall man must be Dimitri, six-foot-five-inches wasn't average "tall" height, and he said that he sees us.

That must mean Myles felt what Dimitri was capable of. And Dimitri must've figured out I was there. Did he know with whom I had gone off with? Did he know I was coming to Portland? And if so, had the Anova's figured that out? *Find him, he is in danger.*

Reading that made my heart stop and stomach drop down to my ankles. All I wanted to do was cry in Dimitri's arms but I couldn't. They had him! Why was this all happening? I decided to get into the shower and just before I did, I caught a glimpse of myself in a full-length mirror.

My body hadn't changed too much, with only being a few months carrying my child, but I did see certain details shifting. My hips got a little wider, no doubt to help with labour. My lower abdomen looked like I was a little bloated and my chest was growing, slightly. My hair had grown out and I decided to let it. It hung just above my hip bones, in a deep cocoa silk wave. Then I looked up to study my face.

Lines of worry and concern, were written all over it. I looked myself in the eyes and could truly see the sadness. Who was I really, trapped in here? Was I some warrior, like I claimed I could be, or was I just a helpless young woman running and pretending, everything was okay? The deep blue of my eyes, started to make me feel like I was drowning in sorrow. Surely, this couldn't be reality. I can connect with nature like no one else I know and I have gifts, but at what cost do they come?

I got into the shower and turned to the water on, extremely hot. I brought my homemade shampoo and soap, and it filled the bathroom, with a clean rose scent. I started to cry, and cry. I sat down, for what felt like two hours but heard a knock on the door.

"Come in!" I shouted, turning the water off and wrapping myself in a towel.

"Hey, Emily. My mom and auntie are back with the food!" said Sophia, clearly happy for her choice, being brought to life.

"Great, thanks, Sof. I'll be down in a minute," I said. When she left, I dried off, got dressed and wrapped my hair up, to dry. With it being so thick, it took forever but I didn't mind, I liked it.

I got downstairs, in time to get a slice, while it was still warm. We decided to stay inside and eat in the living room. It was still chilly enough at night, to catch a cold, if you were to go into the pool, this late.

The living room we sat in, was different than the foyer and my bedroom. It had a very open feeling. Wooden floors stained with cherry red, off-white walls and sage green furniture with white pillows and a bin, filled with throws. Off to the side, was a modern fire place. Someone must've turned it on because I could feel the heat, even before I sat down.

"This is delicious," I commented. I had been so hungry after the road-trip, that this pizza, tasted like love at first sight.

"It's from an Italian owned bakery. I make sure to visit every time I come," said Elizabeth.

After we finished the pizza, I headed off to my room, deciding I deserved to get a well rested sleep because who knows what could happen tomorrow. I needed to be prepared for anything.

The next morning, I woke up more rejuvenated than I had, in a while. Before meeting Sophia and her family, I hadn't realized how lonely, I truly felt. Opening up to people and trusting them, was one of the hardest things for me, so I didn't have that many friends. Dimitri, my parents and his parents, were really the only people, I have opened up to. Even his aunt, Sylvia, I hadn't spoken much too, even though she would ask me questions, all day long.

Thinking about her, made me realize I should stop by and let her know, that I was back in town. I also needed a place to stay. I decided that was the task I could do today, after breakfast of course.

I got dressed, and left my hair down. It had a nice wave to it from my sleep.

"Good morning," all three of them greeted me, as I entered the brilliant kitchen. They all sat at the big marble island, in the middle, and a scent of vanilla hung in the air.

"Good morning, oh, is that french toast?" I asked, eyeing a stack of delicious smelling bread, and practically falling down the stairs.

"Yes, please eat. We have quite as an exciting day, ahead of us. We're planning to head downtown for some shopping and massages," said Elizabeth, as she winked at the last part.

"If you can get a massage. I'm not sure if it's a good idea, while pregnant but we can see," said Victoria, unflinching. My hand, that had been reaching for the french toast, suddenly dropped, as did my throat to my stomach. I felt their eyes studying me, so I tried to appear normal. But, we all knew how easy that was for me.

"Oh, uh… how did you know? I didn't think it was obvious yet," I asked, voice shaking.

"I'm a mom, I know when I see one." that came from Victoria.

"Oh, congratulations! Do you know if it's a boy or a girl? How far along are you? Where's the father? Is he around?" asked Sophia, even more excited than she almost always was – if you could believe it.

"Let her sit down to eat Sophia, I'm sure she's hungry." Victoria pointed to a chair as a command and I followed. Somehow this french toast, seemed less appealing.

"I have to make a call, I'll be back in a minute. It's my husband, I forgot to mention how long we'd be gone for, excuse me," Elizabeth said as she got up and walked away from the table, rolling her eyes.

"So, Emily, are you excited?" Victoria asked me after I finally took a bite of the food.

"I'm…. nervous. I'm not quite sure what will happen. In what aspect?"

"Well, the father is kind of, away right now and I'm not sure when he will be back. A lot of things are on hold for me, now that this has happened, and honestly, I'm a little…. frightened," I said, blown away at myself for even opening up a fraction. What I really wanted to do, was start to cry, but I was on a mission.

"I'm sure everything will work out the way it was meant to. be. Just have some faith," she said as she put a hand over mine and smiled with her soul coming through.

I smiled in return, feeling a little uneasy but happy she was truthful. I didn't want to be a burden but the motherly love was going a long way for me.

"Thank you. I need to run a little errand today on the other side of town. Would it be okay, if I slipped away for about an hour?" I asked the both of them.

"Do you need a ride?" asked Sophia

"No, I'm okay, I can take the subway, I'll be fast and then meet you downtown?"

"Sure," said Victoria, "Call us when you're on the way."
"Oh, uh, I don't actually have a cell phone... I, kinda forgot it, when I left my aunt's and haven't bothered to get a new one." By bothered I meant I didn't want to be tracked.
"You'd better take Sophia, with you then, she has a phone. Plus, two is better, than one," she declared and I wasn't up for arguing.

It would be nice to have a partner, though I hardly wanted her involved with any of this. There was always a way to work around it, and I planned to have Sophia wait, while I checked in to Sylvia's.

Seize the day they say!

4. Betrayal

We took the subway, close to the neighbourhood, where Sylvia's house was. When we got off, I took Sophia on a detour, just to make sure there weren't any Anova's around. She didn't know the difference, so it didn't appear like an odd choice. I wore a baseball cap with a big NY on it, paired with sunglasses and a larger sweater with spandex shorts, stopping just above my knee. On this nice sunny day, with a chill to it, I didn't stand out and it offered me the identity protection I needed.

"Okay, so the house is just around the corner, but I need to check something out, before I go over there. Stay here while I look." I spoke gently and quietly to Sophia.

"Are you like, trying to break in? Why are you whispering?" she asked, with a little humour in her voice, mixed with nervousness.

"No, I just want to make sure no one I don't like is there." A true enough statement, which was met by a shrug and an "ahhh" moment, from Sophia. I left her, to do a quick, around the corner check, to where her mansion sat, in between two other enormous homes. I was close to the trail Dimitri and I had walked, to this path.

From the path, I could peer inside of the yard and check the perimeter. I went down the path, trying my best to keep casual and quiet, while doing so. Usually, Dimitri and I would leave the path, to go further into the forest, that led to a view of the river. It was one of our favourite places to go, and I'm certain it's where we conceived. I finally got to the backyard and peaked in, while pretending to tie my sneaker. Sylvia had cameras, but I knew where they all were.

Part of the instinct in Dimitri, was to always keep a mental note of each buildings layout, exits, and security. I always picked on him because of it, but I paid attention to every word he said, and boy was I ever grateful now.

I looked around and saw nothing. Her dogs weren't outside either, which surprised me. I couldn't remember a time when they were ever in the house, when we lived there. I decided to go around the front to check for cars.

This path led to another path, that would lead me from the west side of the house, to the east side. It was incredibly convenient. I walked normally to the east side and came to a halt, when I could see the driveway through the trees, that engulfed the front yard. When I first saw them, I was happy about the privacy and now I wasn't such a big fan. I again, pretended to tie my shoe and heard a door shut.

I looked over, to see two men getting out of a black SUV. They were met by Sylvia's maid, Amanda. Amanda handed them a piece of paper and said, "She wants this handled, now," then turned and walked away.

The men stood there, for a minute and I got a better look at them. One had his back towards me but was tall. Maybe six-foot-two-inches, and the other was noticeably shorter, by a few inches.

I took in every detail of the man, with his back to me and I could see a tattoo, on his left hand. It was a geometric shape I couldn't remember the name of and covered his entire hand. He wore a black suit, so seeing that kind of tattoo, made me think, he wasn't in a business of, say, real-estate. His geometric hand shifted slightly and my breath caught.

The shorter man, was the same one I had recognized, when the crow brought me the vision of the Anova's at my cabin. He was bald and older, maybe in his early-forties, but looked evil.

His eyes looked black and his face had one large scar, from the right side, down to the chin. It looked like the grim reaper, would've been scared of him. I moved slightly, so that I wouldn't be seen.

I tried to think of a reason, this short bald guy would be at Sylvia's house? Why had Amanda not been afraid? I was thirty-feet away and terrified. I racked my brain and tried to figure out where I had seen him before, but nothing came up. I got up and walked back toward the path, then heard Sylvia herself from her office window. "You cannot be serious!" she exclaimed, "How hard is it for you to do one job? Why even hire you, when I could've handled this myself with less screw-ups!"

She hung up, by slamming the phone against the table. "Ma'am, would you like tea?" asked someone. I wasn't quite sure, maybe a new maid.

"No. What I want is for you to finish cleaning out the girl's room and find me anything of value. She must be somewhere!" Sylvia exclaimed.

"Ma'am we cleaned it out already, and all the items have been checked. There's nothing there. We put everything in storage like you asked."

"There is no way a twenty-two-year-old witch, can hide this well. Find something. Find ANYTHING. Do you know how long the Anova's have been around? How long I'VE been around, Susan, do you?"

"Uh, no ma'am." replied the strange voice, with a shake to it.

"Thousands of years, eradicating the world of witches and their magic. We have wiped out most clans but some remain. And do you know why they remain? Hmm? Do you? Because people like Jeff, and John who can't do their jobs! You know why we do this. You understand why the mission is important, correct?" Sylvia was practically irate.

I had never heard that kind of tone from her before... It was so cold.

"Yes, ma'am. So, your nephew isn't caught with a witch."

"Uh-huh, and what else?"

"To make sure their magic is lost."

"Exactly! The world doesn't need magic, the world needs to be cleansed of those people. Now, go make me a tea. And get Dimitri on the phone."

I was sure my heartbeat was in my throat and I knew standing out here, was only putting myself in line, for more danger. I should get out of here, but I was too shocked. All of the things in this world... Sylvia... Dimitri.

I heard the phone dial, and then the sweetest sound in the entire world.

"Hello?" I gasped. It was Dimitri's voice. Laced with a slight Greek accent. He sounded exhausted.

"Hi, it's your aunt. No luck finding anything yet?" She asked in a much nicer tone than the one she used with Susan. I cringed at hearing the act.

"No ma'am, we haven't been able to find her. I'm starting to get worried."

"Relax nephew, she must be fine. I've got my best search party looking for her. Come home and rest for a week. I've asked the Nelson's, to bring others in for overtime."

Come home?

A sudden ruffle in the trees made me nearly leap out of my skin. I saw Sophia coming out of them and ran towards her. I tackled her back into the trees, away from the security camera. Safe for her identity, plus we could not risk getting caught.

"What are you doing?" She hissed, as I rolled off of her but kept a hand on her shoulder, to keep her down. "People I don't like, are here, you won't like them either. Best to keep you safe." I whispered.

How good was tackling for the baby? I didn't feel anything and I hardly put a lot of effort into it. Sophia may be tall, but she was very thin and at an easy weight to push.

"So, you tackle me to the ground!? What is wrong with you," she asked, as she pushed to sit up. I let her.

"Nothing. Lets go"

I helped her up and then we jogged our way back to the subway station. We called her family and met the two women downtown. They were shopping at a designer shop I had never heard of.

"Sophia, why are you full of dirt?" Her mother asked upon our arrival.

"Oh, I tripped over a tree root," she said, only briefly meeting my eyes. I looked like I had seen a ghost but tried to mask it with a happy look instead.

Victoria shook her head comically, and then turned to me, "Did you go and see your aunt?"

"She wasn't home," I lied. What a lousy lie, I guess. "No, I think she's plotting to have me murdered," sounded too blunt.

"Too bad. Check out this dress!" piped in Elizabeth, holding up a colourful piece that would fit her brilliantly.

I stepped out, to get some fresh air. I began to nervously pace in front of the store, almost burning holes, in my sneakers.

"Okay, so, so, so, so, so, so," I said aloud to myself, not caring if anyone was looking or heard me. I needed to think this through. I needed to organize and draw a map. I went back into the designer store, and asked for a pen and paper. They handed it to me and I went back out.

"Okay, this is what we know," I said, as I started to scribble on the paper. "ME," I wrote at the top. Then, I wrote about the Anova's and what day they found the camp. I then wrote about the two men I had seen at Sylvia's, with detailed descriptions about their appearances.

Then, I wrote down what I overheard Sylvia saying to that other lady, Susan. I wrote, Amanda knew and added in, that they cleaned out my room and put my stuff in storage. I looked up at the sky and took a deep breath. There were a few things, I knew for sure.

One, Sylvia was in on having death brought to my front door step.

Two, Dimitri didn't know anything that was going on but was being summoned back home.

And three, I was terrified and confused on what to do next. I called to one of my ancestors. Even though, I was in the middle of a city, in broad daylight on a sidewalk, I didn't care. I needed the help.

"Elayo, Elayo, please come. Come to me" I whispered. When I didn't feel anything after a few minutes, I spoke in an old tongue, I somehow knew, "Elayo, ichbar itu ichbar."

My child.

Finally, Elayo arrived. "Elayo I need your help. I'm lost. Where do I go?"

Go, where you have never gone before. Where the road leads to a dead end. You must go there, for that will be the place you conquer your enemies.

"How will I conquer them, Elayo? I'm so scared." It just barely came out in a whisper, and I fought tears.

Child. Some things, are left for the gods to understand. They say, 'illubi a shami fur elitar' to you. You will know what it means when the time is right.

"And when is that?"

You will know.

Elayo said as his voice faded away. I have never been able to see my ancestors but I desperately wanted to. Having them leave cryptic messages like this, was pure agony and I was upset that they didn't help me further. I was dealing with life and death and if they wanted me to come here to make a change, shouldn't they be helping me? How dare they disappear when I needed them the most.

After twenty or so minutes, the ladies came out and we stopped to pick some food up before heading back to our rented home. We sat and ate together but I didn't pay much attention to anyone. I was hungry, upset, and about to break into hysteria. The night went by quickly and I decided to head to bed early.

I couldn't take any more of reality today, and a part of me wished I was dead already.

That night I dreamt of my son. Him and I were in some land, I didn't recognize, and he kept screaming for help.

I was paralyzed and couldn't move towards him in his crib. He kept jumping up and down, screaming in pain and he looked at me laying on the floor. I looked over beside the crib and saw two men in suits looking at him, while he screamed at them. They reached out to grab him and even though he was a baby, he fought so hard to get away.

Eventually the men got him, and took him. I started to cry in the dream but I couldn't move or feel anything, just a broken heart. I kept wanting to scream, "My son, my son, leave my son alone."

I woke up, drenched in sweat. I looked around the room, moving my hands and feet to make sure I was okay. I let my hand wander down to my belly and felt it was fine. The clock over to my right, was blinking three-thirty-three AM and I wondered if I could possibly continue with sleep, after what had just happened.

I eventually, drifted back into sleep but heard a wolf's howl, at some point in the night. It made me wonder if there was a coincidence to that, or if we were just close enough to some den in the trees.

My sleep ended, when I heard the birds chirping. I looked at my clock once again and saw, six-fifty-four AM.

"I guess it's as good of a time to get up as ever," I said, as I rolled over and put my slippers on. The house had come with an extraordinary amount of amenities, which included slippers, bathrobes and an all you could drink bar. I didn't have the luxury of drinking from it, but believe me, did I ever want to. If I wasn't carrying this baby, I would've had my way, with a bottle of Crown Royal already.

I showered and got ready for the day, pausing in the mirror to take in my changing body. I could see the little bump, but it wasn't anything large enough, to need to buy new clothes. Today, was supposed to be very warm and humid, so I put on a pair of waist high, loose jean shorts and one of Dimitri's t-shirts. It was very oversized on me, so it was great in the heat.

Sadly, it no longer smelled like his beautiful scent of sandalwood, with a hint of geranium. Looking at it, made me spiral, into an even darker mood. I went downstairs to eat, and was relieved that no one was awake yet.

The rooms in the house were spread apart enough, that moving about wouldn't create too much noise, giving me the freedom to cook. I was feeling light headed, so I decided to cook some of the wild meat I had brought with me. I figured, if I was going to continue living, I had to be strong in body, mind and soul.

Breakfast seemed like a good opportunity, to work on my body. After breakfast, I did some yoga to try and ease my mind. I didn't bother to change my clothes, I just went in the backyard and took them off, allowing me the complete freedom of body movement.

I was so into the flow, of the movement, that I could feel the energy in my body moving around. Some was stuck in my muscles and I had to work extra hard, to get the darker energy out. I hadn't realized how much weight I had been carrying in me, but it was a lot more, then one person should be able to handle.

"Looks like you're feeling a lot better," I turned and met Victoria peering at me through the patio door.

"Yes, sometimes I get too wrapped up in my head that I neglect my body. It feels better when I move," I said, demonstrating the movement in my arms, then realized I was naked. Shocked at the situation, I grabbed my shirt and pulled it over my head, "Oops, I guess I should've left it on." I said, as I pulled up my shorts.

"Well, I am a mom. Nothing I haven't seen before. Coffee? Decaf?" She called behind her as she walked back into the house.

"Sure." I replied.

I walked back in and sat at the island, watching Victoria make a fresh pot. She made me feel comfortable, which didn't happen around a lot of people.

"Did you eat already? It smells good down here," she said as she placed a full cup in front of me.

"Yeah, I did. I wasn't sure if I should make some, for everyone. I didn't know if you'd be up. Sorry."

"No need to apologize" she said, with a smile that was very genuine.

We sat in silence for a bit, as she looked around the groceries we bought yesterday. Meanwhile, I battled with an inner dialogue. I had a big problem on my hands and didn't know if I could handle it on my own. I certainly felt like I was already dead, but didn't want to go down, without at least trying. Sylvia said she had thousands of years of experience and what did I have? Twenty-two years, and a three-month-old embryo growing inside of me, with less hope than I had started with.

The only people I have ever trusted were no where near me now, and I couldn't risk putting them in danger. It was hard for me to even imagine letting new people in, as betrayal wasn't a foreign concept to me. Almost my entire life I have been screwed over by someone from being too open and naive about the world.

To me, we live on a beautiful planet, full of magic and joy. But to others, we live on a wasteland, ready to take whatever, for their own gain while others suffer.

Looking at Victoria now, I really did see how nice she was. Her aura came to me in strong colours. I didn't want to get her into any trouble but certainly could use a little bit of help. My logic started to weigh in, more and more, and I decided if I was going to chance my life, I could also chance my heart.

"So, uh, how long are you guys staying in town again?" I asked, knowing it was only a few more days, but I needed to start this conversation somewhere.

"Were here until Friday. Then it's back to Olympia," replied Victoria, dryly. Making it seem like she didn't actually like it there.

"Did the renter say if anyone was coming right after? I saw some people at my aunt's yesterday, that I don't like, so I would rather just stay here for a bit longer until they leave." I spoke with a casual air, not wanting to give away my desperation.

"I can give her a call, I'm sure she won't mind. It's actually my great aunt's house, but she moved to the Maldives."

"Wow! What, I wouldn't give to do that." I said, with a little envy. What a nice life, to have a mansion here, move to the Maldives and still make money renting it out. I made a mental note, that if I made it through this, that would be om my bucket list.

"You and I both know, you don't like to run from your problems," she said with a stern face, but then caught herself and said, "I don't mean to come off as intrusive."

"No, it's fine, I've been sort of an enigma since arriving on your front door step, so I would like to be open and honest with you now. But, uh, please don't judge me too much, or think I'm totally insane. I mean, I sound crazy but it's just because these things, usually don't happen to normal people..." and then I went on, explaining everything that was going on.

I left out a few details, but otherwise, I told her most of my abilities. After I finished, I realized I was in tears talking about everything. Just like with yoga, I felt more of that dark energy around me, leave, and I felt... relieved.

Victoria didn't say anything, but she handed me a tissue. At one point, I started to hyperventilate and she touched my hand and squeezed it. After about twenty minutes, of a rare full display of my emotions, I took a deep breath and relaxed.

I stared at my hands, terrified to look at her because if she didn't believe me and kicked me out, I would be even more broken. That was something I didn't want to endure.

"It sounds like you have quite a few things on your plate and I have an idea on how to help."

I immediately jerked my head up, to look at her, to see if she was displaying any kind of trickery. She wasn't. Her face was serious, but warm and her jade eyes glowed more than I had ever seen.

"Okay, what are you thinking?" Feeling more relieved, by her willingness to help. Prior to her reply, I really thought I had gone insane, and was lost in my own misery for the rest of eternity.

"Well, you said Dimitri is coming back to Portland, to rest for a week? Let's get his attention, without getting caught. If we can catch him in the streets and pass him a note, then we can get him out of there without getting hurt. No one knows you're here, which gives us a head start. But, even better, no one knows my family and I even exist. It gives you the perfect opportunity, to remain a ghost but get things done." She placed her hands, neatly folded on the island, like a lawyer would after presenting case facts. She was impressive.

I felt a thousand thoughts move through my mind, not in a linear fashion, but all at once. I pondered this. If I could get a head start on the Anova's, then that would mean I could save myself, and Dimitri from an awful fate. Maybe I wouldn't have to fight to the death and Elayo's advice, was just to meet somewhere and run off together. This could work and be simple.

"That's genius, Victoria. But it is essential you and your family stay out of harms way, okay?" I told her in a stern manner.

I didn't want to risk any of them, so minimal contact and attention would be the best-case scenario. She nodded.

"Alright, I'll make a plan today and then I'll explain everything to the others." I told her.

She nodded again and then we sat there in silence, off in our own thoughts. I wondered if she had been through something similar, and understood the need to protect your loved ones. I had met this stranger, three days ago, and here she stood, ready to help me with all my life problems. The annoying hum of an inner voice crept in and with its anxiety, presenting questions I didn't want to ask.

   Why did she care so much? Why does she want to help someone like me? Can she be trusted? Where is Sophia's father? Is he in on it? I had to get up and move or else I would soon suffocate under the pressure these thoughts had. My chest began to feel as if it could tighten to the point of breaking, while piercing my heart, with an end of a broken bone.

   I went up to my room and decided it would be a good idea to strategize everything out. If I wanted this done, I had to make sure there was no room for error. If Sylvia hadn't caught me by now, there was clearly a reason and I wasn't about to give her an edge, to this chess match.

   I would win.

   I passed Elizabeth in the hall on the way to my room and she looked like she had been dragged in, by a cat.

   "Good morning, Elizabeth, how are you?" I asked as politely as I could. I was afraid speaking too loudly might scare her off.

   "Morning" she said with eyes that appeared to register nothing around her. She seemed numb, and it didn't feel right.

   I looked at Elizabeth and decided I could risk a hug. I went in and wrapped my arms around her tightly, sending all the happy thoughts I could muster up, "I hope you feel better," I whispered in her ear.

After a few seconds I pulled away, collecting all the data I needed, by looking into her eyes. She gave me a weak smile, nodded and then headed off downstairs, towards the kitchen. Elizabeth was less soulful than Victoria but I had already picked that up.

It didn't mean she was a bad person, it just meant she was less connected to her higher-self, which essentially, is her soul.

"Wow, why are you in such deep thought?" I heard a voice but didn't quite register it, important enough for a reply. I just stood there, looking off into the distance, pondering existence.

A light tap on my shoulder, snapped me out of it. I felt Sophia's energy mix into mine and was caught off guard.

With my abilities, it was easy for me to morph with others. I could feel what they felt, as if I was them. If I wasn't careful, in keeping myself shielded, I become a different person.

It was weird. Her energy was light, but laced with concern, as she regarded me, with her deep brown eyes. I turned to look at her and relaxed my body. I contemplated telling her about the revelations, about her aunt but decided on another time.

"Were out of maple syrup, so I can't have waffles today," I said, deciding a light hearted joke was better. She seemed not to buy it, but decided to shrug and smile when I didn't further explain.

"I never knew you would be willing to contemplate life for waffles but hey, who am I to judge?" she chuckled.

"You've clearly never had waffles in Belgium before. I'm about to go get ready for the day, I'll meet you downstairs in thirty?" I said to her, smiling.

"Okie dokie" she sang out as she skipped down the stairs like a lanky fairy. The resemblance between her and her mother was uncanny at this point and I enjoyed seeing the other, in both of them.

I went to my room and started to brainstorm. I started with the facts. I had help from an unknown source, plus Dimitri was on his way back to town. Sylvia had called more of the Anova's, to come and find me, so perhaps they would all be meeting at Sylvia's.

I needed to find that out for sure. I summoned up my energy and felt a light tickle run through my body. I used my higher vibration, to manifest an animal, that could be helpful to my cause. Usually, they found me when they needed to but now, I had to learn how to bring them to me at will.

Animals were harder to manifest because they were a real being, with their own feelings and personality. Some individual animals, didn't like me as much, to come close enough for me to touch.

So, I had to call to the ones, who fit into my energy level. It was all very complicated, and probably could be explained in a physics formula – if only everyone believed in the link, between mind and universe.

I stood there, thinking of the right animal for me. I thought of the specific tasks I would need it to do, and how courageous the tasks were. My focus became so intense, that I felt nothing around me. My body didn't even feel real enough, to be standing by a window, but rather just a mind, floating in the air, like a cloud on a bright and sunny day.

The intensity grew and I felt a white light flash through my body, like a magnet pulling from the core of the earth into the heavens. I stood there, stunned by the light and feeling more like the flow, than ever before in my life. I felt true bliss in this moment and never wanted it to end.

I heard something hit the window and my eyes flew open. Any floating of energy was gone, but I felt a slight hum coursing through my veins, the only indication of what had just happened. I peaked around and saw a little sparrow, clinging onto the side of the brown toned brick beside it. I popped open the screen and held my hand out. The sparrow looked at it, then me, and then flew to land, on my shaking index finger.

The light that flowed through me earlier, took me by surprise and I was still trying to calm down.

"Hey there little buddy, aren't you just the cutest of them all," I said to the little sparrow. I knew these birds were feisty, but they were just so cute up close, that I wondered if this was really the right animal for the mission.

"Are you sure you're the one for me?" I asked in a tone, that sounded like I was speaking to a baby.

The sparrow looked at me, and I swear, rolled his eyes. He tilted his head, to get a better look and then flew around the room.

Out of instinct, I ducked away from him, and crouched to the floor. Watching this deranged thing flying around me, dangerously close to the ceiling fan, in and out of the bathroom and then landing on my bed, right above where I was crouched. He looked at me again, with a hard look and I kneeled up to face this tiny being.

I reached out again, with my hand.

I may not be as mighty as the wolf, or the bear but I can do things, they can't. Things you will need. Do not insult my courage, with mockery. I heard in my mind.

This little guy definitely had a leader attitude. I shouldn't have judged him, considering I didn't even believe all too much in myself, right now.

"I'm sorry. Thank you for honouring me, with your help," I said to him, "here's what I need," and I revealed the plan to him. He nodded as his way of approval and flew out of the middle pane window, off to get it done.

5. Dimitri

The day went by in a blur. Victoria had told the others that I needed their help and they were in. She hadn't mentioned how severe the situation was, or that I was a witch, which I appreciated. I didn't mention to her that I didn't want everyone knowing, but I think my apprehensiveness to even tell her, was an indication that details could be left out.

They asked me simple things like what I knew about Dimitri's return, which I answered that I figured by the end of the day, he would be back. They also asked why Sylvia had it out for me, which I met that answer with, the fact that she doesn't think I'm right for her nephew.

Sophia asked who the men were, the day we went to look at my old house, and I told her I didn't know them that well but they frightened me. That was the truth and that was the part that bothered me the most. I recognized one of them but I still couldn't remember and it bugged me.

Maybe if I could recall, this would be an easier puzzle to solve.

I decided to cook that night, and made a zucchini lasagna for everyone. I loved the kitchen so much, that I even made homemade affogatos. Doing something mundane like this, really helped my mind work through its problems. The thing about coming back to a society with such high pressure, was that it was easy to forget the simple ways of life.

Instead of waking up everyday and meditating, for as long as my body needed, I would wake up and have a ten-minute hot shower, to ease tension instead. It wasn't nearly as effective and it was something I had always struggled with, my entire life. Normal society, versus all the things that go on in my head and how to deal with it. It was a real bitch.

We finished eating and we were sitting around the table, playing a game of crazy eight's. I had always enjoyed card games and it wasn't something Dimitri could always beat me in – though he never went down easily. "Wow, look at you go. Are you counting the cards?" He had asked me one day, when I was beating him effortlessly.

"Perhaps. We're on a yacht, not in Vegas so I think its fair game, no?" I asked with a sly smirk on my face. I knew, he knew, I was counting them, but I loved to tease. He says he fell in love with me, for my heart and my mind, but I say it was for my sass and wit.

"Hurry up and beat me then, so we can get on with the real fun," he said, giving me a look of hunger. It didn't look like he wanted to play, but he knew exactly what he was playing for. Those rare smirks when he would play devil-may-care always made my heart rate increase, a thousand percent.

I remember feeling my blood boil and rush through my body up to my face, illustrating just how hard my heart beat for him. I don't think we even finished the game that day.

"Your go, Emily" said Sophia. Dragging me back to this game. I didn't want to count the cards this time, but it was so easy for me, that I had already won a few rounds.

I decided to play down my turn and placed a card I knew would be met by Victoria, with the two of spades, instead of showing off and winning. In turn, she threw down the two, and Elizabeth let out an, "oh dang!" It was adorable to watch them all together, and I truly felt like I was in a safe space. So safe in fact, that I no longer wanted to go by a fake name.

    I actually couldn't stand the name Emily, because it wasn't who I was. I'm Emilia Diomades, Warrior of Earth, end of story.

    Sophia just played the card, I knew she would drop. It was a Jack of Spades and I used it as an opportunity to play the other three Jack's, using the Jack of hearts, then placed my Queen of Hearts last. They all put the in cards down and stared at me, astonished.

    "How do you do that?" asked Victoria, as she placed the fairy, filled with wonder in her hands, with a contemplative look.

    "I count the cards, naturally," I said. They looked as if I told them I hit an old lady with my car. I simply met their looks, with a shrug, "they make it too easy for me. I clean up in Vegas. We'll go and I'll show you sometime," I said with a triumphant smile.

    Vegas, is actually where I got enough money, to do whatever I wanted with. I ended up gambling so good, that I won close to a million dollars. I then used that money and put it into investments, here in the United States, Canada, Greece and Dubai. From there it was simply moving the money around, to avoid the government as much as possible and I ended up with close to thirty-million. Don't ask me how, but I guess being linked with source also means unlimited abundance.

"How did you not get arrested?" Sophia asked wide-eyed. I felt like I was becoming more and more of a bad-ass in her eyes, which was a good thing. I always felt like I wasn't.

"Dimitri is a pretty big guy. I think the security wanted to avoid getting into it with him."

"Awesome." All three of them said together.

"Oh hey, uh, I have to tell you all. My name isn't Emily, that's just the name I've been going by since all this stuff happened. My real name is Emilia. I prefer that name," I said nervously. I really didn't like being open with anyone but every time I was, I felt more and more of that dense energy leaving, making me feel freer and freer.

"Emilia, that's a beautiful name," Elizabeth said with a smile.

"Yeah, I like it a lot!" exclaimed Sophia.

"Ah yes, Emilia. It suits your artistic look," said Victoria. I liked that compliment the most.

Dimitri had always said, I looked like "poetry in motion" and I missed hearing those words. Lately I felt like poetry on a piece of paper, that was crumbled up, stomped on, half-burned, and then drenched with two day old coffee.

"You guys are taking me very well. I didn't expect such...niceness from strangers? I mean, I really appreciate it. But why are you all so great? If everyone was like you, it would make the world a much better place filled with less judgement." I asked them.

Really, they were the nicest people I had ever met. Almost too nice, and to the point where I felt like maybe this was all a facade. I didn't want that little voice of skepticism, to take over my thoughts, but I had to ask. It was an itch, I had to scratch.

It took a minute for them to think. They all looked at each other, with a knowing look, that made me feel out of the loop.

"Well..." started Victoria, then Sophia piped in to take charge of the way this was going to go. I hadn't thought of her as an assertive person, but she really impressed me with the leadership quality.

"My dad was murdered a couple years ago in New York. They were never able to catch the person who did it, and it haunts us. Always wondering who took him, why they took him and if they'll find us. We moved from there to Olympia, where my auntie was living already, just in case. It's been hard on all of us."

"It was shocking and very painful. We don't want you to go through the same thing as us and if we can help, we will," Victoria said ending Sophia's thoughts. I was shocked at the news. They all seemed strong and well put together.

Victoria's only sign of age, was a few grey hairs with light signs of crow's feet by her eyes. Other than that, I hadn't been able to notice any signs of stress. Sophia was always so happy and ready to lend a hand to anyone near her. I've never noticed sadness, but then again, she had a lot more soul in her eyes, than any other seventeen-year-old, I had ever encountered.

As for Elizabeth, I just thought she held sadness, because of some other reason, but maybe her brother-in-law's death was the main cause. This revelation, really showed me, that even with all my powers, I still didn't know everything and should be a better listener.

"Oh, I'm so sorry to hear that... I really wish that had never happened to any of you, for you are all such wonderful people and I value you in my life. I couldn't imagine... even the thought of......" I couldn't finish the sentence, but they knew what I meant.

They all got up and came to hug me, as I sat in my chair sobbing. I cried softly and allowed them to hold me in a group hug for a lot longer than most people's hands, have touched me. I shielded my energy, but also allowed some light to go from me to them and vice versa. Hoping to allow the healing of some wounds, internal or external. It didn't matter, as long as, after this hug, we all felt better.

They let go, and sat back down again. I cleaned my face with the bathrobe, I had been wearing and smiled at them all, as a way of a thank-you and a sorry-for-balling.

No one even batted an eye at my outburst, and we all talked, for what felt like hours. Elizabeth was the first to go to bed, but even after that, the three of us sat, for another hour or so. When we looked and saw it was half past midnight, we knew it was time for rest. Tomorrow was the day our plan began and we all needed some rest.

We all headed off to bed, but before I went to my room, Sophia caught a hold of my robe.

"Hey, Emil-er-Emilia? Could you teach me how to count cards? I want to gamble and make some money to be able to help-my mom out. She works so hard, and does so much for me, that winning a bunch of money would really help us out. What do you think?" She asked with beaming eyes, like within me were all the answers to her long-lost needs to contribute to her mother.

They were so full with life and compassion that it hurt me to even think of saying no to her.

"Counting cards is dangerous you know. You would have to listen to every single thing I say and maybe even learn some combat moves just in case you get into trouble. People don't like to see their money leave their hands." I told her with a stern look. I hoped this came across as serious. It was like I was in training to be a mom, while also getting a chance to be a sister again.

"I promise to listen to everything you say. I'll even take notes!"

I chuckled.

"No notes, the point is not to get caught, so just remember everything. I'll teach you once this is all over and everything is settled. Okay?"

"Deal! Thank you Emily-er-Emilia!" she said as she flung her arms around me in a quick hug. She pulled away, smiled and went off into her room.

I wondered, if I just got the both of us into trouble, or if I could actually teach someone what I thought was a natural talent. I agreed because I didn't think you could actually learn how to count cards, but what if I just signed up to giving life long lessons? If she didn't learn, I would just give her a chunk of money and teach her how to invest. I was probably going to do that anyways, if this mission was a success – or even if not.

I wanted to pay them back in whatever way I could, so if money was needed, then money was what they were going to get. I was awakened early in the morning, by the sparrow I had sent out. He picked at my window, and sang until I was awake enough to walk over and let him in. I still hadn't put the screen back on the window, specifically for this reason. He flew in and this time went for the mahogany dresser. He sat up there, looking at me with a knowing look. I saw life in this bird's eyes, that went beyond just a tiny sparrow.

"So, Jack, what do you have for me?" I liked Johnny Depp, so if I had a pet sparrow, it had to be Jack. I didn't hear any of his thoughts and decided to go closer. I put my hand up, allowing him space to hop onto my index finger, and he did. I allowed myself to open up and hear him.

Dimitri is back. I heard him talking about going to his favourite cafe this morning. Jack spoke to me in my mind. I always wondered if an animal would talk aloud to me, then always dismissed the thought. How weird could earth really get?

"Do you know what time?" I asked. It was five-fifteen this morning already and I knew Dimitri was an early riser.

He just woke up. I flew over to let you know.

I cursed. I felt my heart beat begin to speed up and suddenly felt extremely nauseous. I knew this was what I wanted, but now that I had to do this, it seemed so big... so intimidating.

Was I capable of pulling this off, or was I about to lead the four of us into a death trap? The pressure made me feel sick, like my stomach was churning, over acidic slime, while eating my insides.

Jack chirped at me and I snapped out of my spiral. I looked him in the eyes and saw an amount of seriousness, deep in the tiny beads of black. He was lending me strength, I realized. I took a deep breath and exhaled, while putting Jack back on the dresser.

"Okay, the plan starts now. Jack, you remember what told you, right?"

He nodded his head and looked at me for a few seconds to confirm he understood the assignment.

"Good. I'll see you tomorrow morning. Be safe," I said, as I pulled some sunflower seeds, out of the dresser drawer. I fed them to him, for about a minute, then he flew back out the window.

After a quick hot shower, I paused to study my body again. Everyday I would see little details, that would change and I found it fascinating. Another human was growing inside of me, feeding off of my nutrients, downloading DNA from both me and the father. I couldn't help but be in awe, at the process and really hoped I could soon relax and enjoy it in a normal setting.

Today, my lower abs looked like they were carrying an avocado inside of them. I saw a bit of a stretch marks coming on to my side and I was saddened by the way my skin was changing. I observed from all angles and made sure to lotion everything. Perhaps all I needed was hydration inside and out.

I put on an outfit that wasn't mine, but was Sophia's. She lent me clothes, figuring it would be good for me, to dress differently on this mission, and to be able to do all my laundry – the laundry part, was why I agreed. She let me borrow jean overall's, with a long sleeve cotton burgundy shirt, to put underneath the denim. It was a nice contrast and they fit loose enough, to fit my growing hips in, but tight enough that you could see some curves. I actually liked this look and the colour contrast was outstanding.

A rich, deep burgundy, contrasted with a light denim on top. It was like a form of the yin-yang but in fashion. I paired this with white sneakers and tied my hair into a bun at my neck. I took some strands of wanna-be bangs and put them in front of my face. I studied myself, for a long time, seriously, while staring into my eyes and repeating something, Dimitri always used to tell me.

"If you get knocked down nine times, you get up ten," he would say. Always with compassion in his deep eyes, that resembled a forest. Unwavering from his seriousness, while delivering messages, he was the perfect image of love. Hard at times, when you needed to be pushed, but soft when he knew you needed a moment.

I had so many mixed feelings, about seeing him today. Part of me, just wanted to stay here and let the others do the task, but I knew I had to be there, no matter how much it hurt. I knew I had to protect them.

I went downstairs and to my surprise, everyone was already up. Breakfast today was eggs, bacon, and toast.

Two foods that I wouldn't touch, unless my life depended on it. I walked up to the fridge, to see what else there was and to my astonishment, there was a stack of waffles, waiting for me, beside it.

"OH! You made waffles! And look, pure maple syrup right from the tree," I said, grabbing the plate, and turning around to look at them all, wide-grinned.

"Thought that might get you through the day," said Victoria stuffing scrambled eggs in her mouth. She looked up and met my eyes, smiling with chipmunk cheeks.

I wasted no time sitting down and stuffing food into my body. I loved waffles so much and they always reminded me of my time, backpacking Europe. I went on my own, shortly after graduating there and tried waffles, in every country I went to. It was a food most places had on their menu and even though I loved food in general, waffles were always, consistently great. They tasted like pure sunshine, mixed with the holiness of a sweet tree, oozing with greatness. It was a small thing, but meant the world to me.

We finished up eating and I told them where Dimitri would be, this morning.

"How do you know for sure?" asked Sophia.

"I have my sources," I told her, with one of my sly smiles. I rarely was ever playful and I missed being like that. I used to be fun. I guess life had just punched me so many times, I changed. But as Dimitri says... get up ten.

We headed out and everyone wore casual clothing, with runners on, minimal jewelry and no baggage. It was a specific detail, I had made sure they all understood. If we had to run, we needed to be prepared.

Elizabeth wore dark jeans and a very lovely white blouse. It was beautiful, but loose enough, that it didn't restrict her natural body movements. Her blonde hair was in a high pony tail and she wore big glasses to cover her eyes. She struck me, as the kind of person, that always needed to properly accessorize. However, today, she looked the most casual I had ever seen her.

"You didn't do your makeup this morning, Elizabeth," I said to her, as we were leaving the house.

I wanted to point out, how nice she looked naturally, because I got the feeling, she wasn't told of her beauty often. Or simply didn't believe, she possessed any.

"Yeah, I decided against it. After last night's talk, I just felt like I haven't been myself lately. Today, I wanted to be more me," she finished with a smile as we reached the

Porsche SUV. I returned her smile, with genuine affection in my eyes.

"You sit in the front, Emilia. You have to keep an eye on everything," Victoria told me, as she switched-spots with me, from the passenger side of the car. She, too, looked casual and ready to go in her blue jeans, sage green t-shirt, paired with a cream cardigan. Her light brown curly hair, was pinned back, away from her face, espousing her fairy like features. She wore a look that said, "don't mess with me," and I didn't bother.

I moved into the front seat, ready to deliver the directions. I recapped the plan and told each of them where I wanted them to go and at what times. We all synced our watches, to be exact, and I felt more and more, like I was truly going to succeed today. As I spoke, I radiated confidence and the nervous atmosphere in the car began to shift, to one of empowerment and determination.

I realized that nothing was going to stand in our way today and that was that. Dimitri's favourite place was called Jugando and it was located in Downtown Portland. It was a little hidden café, that looked like just a grocery store. Once you went in and passed the facade of the front, it was the best spot in town, for an authentic Mexican atmosphere.

Spanish was one of my favourite languages to speak. I was totally bummed, that I wouldn't be going in, as my role was to be invisible, until I needed to be seen.

We parked a couple blocks away from Jugando, and went over the details once again.

"Okay, Sophia. He's really easy to spot and will most likely be reading a book. Probably an ancient history novel in English. You remember what I said to say to him, right?" I asked, as we huddle in a circle, semi-whispering.

"Yes, I have to mention the name of your favourite town, to visit in Greece, but make sure it isn't the entire word."

"Yes, exactly. Something like, Thessa, Loniki, Essaloni. Anything similar to that, and he should be able to understand. If not, just say you thought he was someone else and leave. I'll be watching from the roof, to see when he starts to follow you." I turned to Victoria, "You're all good, to make a distraction when he leaves the cafe? It's important to startle as many people close to him, as possible. I need to see if he's being followed."

"Yes, I can create a scene. That's how I got out of being arrested once, in college," she said, with a hint of a smile on her lips. We all took a brief moment to stare at her, stunned at what she just revealed. I liked her more and more everyday. I turned to Elizabeth, who looked a little more, pale, but still determined.

"All you have to do, is bump him into the alley, between Eighth and Broadview. There's the back door there, that leads into a restaurant. He'll follow, if you tell him to. Lead him through the restaurant, out the front door, across the street, and into this parkade. But don't come to the first level, where the car is, go to the second level in the far east corner. It's close enough to the stairs for our escape, while not showing the identity of the car, we have. Got it?"

She nodded. We all came into a group hug and then headed off. I gave them all instructions, on how to look casual yet watch everything. I was nervous for all of them, but I needed to trust their instincts and myself, as a teacher.

I sprinted up to the roof, which was four flights of stairs, but a breeze for me. My anxiety was already pumping out so many endorphins, that I could probably be stabbed and not feel anything for four days.

I got to the rooftop corner, where I was able to watch the entire scene. It was seven-thirty and I knew the cafe was open. If Jack had been right, Dimitri would've arrived fifteen minutes ago, giving him enough time, to get his coffee, sit in his spot and take his book out. I looked at my watch, counting down the seconds. Every passing of the hand, felt like another year went by and I gripped the binoculars I bought, so tightly, my knuckles became translucent.

Tick, tick, tick my watch went like the strangers passing down below. The good thing was that there weren't a lot of people around like there would be around noon. The bad thing was that it wouldn't be extremely easy to blend into a crowd if there wasn't much of one. That's why it was so important to do this plan in stages. I wasn't sure if Dimitri had been followed, but if I was trying to kill someone, I would watch over their loved-ones, knowing they would show up sooner or later.

After five minutes of agony, I saw Sophia come out of the café, holding a small cup close to her mouth, which was the sign, that Dimitri was there. I forgot how to breathe.

A few seconds later, I saw him. The most beautiful human in the entire world, stepped out of the cafe and I felt nothing around me but him and his energy. I saw nothing but him, as he walked cautiously behind Sophia. He looked as deadly as ever, stalking his prey. His body was incredible, amplified by his tight black t-shirt, that showed off how chiseled he was. The fabric clung to him, like I wanted to and he wore black sweats, with his hair in a bun at the neck. He had his book – indeed an ancient history novel – in his left hand and coffee in the right. I felt myself wanting to cry right then and there.

Relentlessly, I pulled my eyes away from him and swept the area. I looked, but saw no one trailing him. I then looked around for cars that could be watching, and again, saw nothing. Maybe I had been wrong?

I found Victoria on the street about six feet behind Dimitri. She 'tripped' and spilled coffee all over herself. I heard her cuss, and boy was she right. She could make a scene. She picked up a tin trash can and threw it against a wall. When the impact startled everyone, I saw two men emerge from around the corner of the café, coming towards her. They were in suits, just like the day I went to Sylvia's.

And just like the day at Sylvia's, they wore that look of death on them. I felt chills run down my spine, almost as if they ran down to the ground, and escape those horrible faces. They went towards her, to try and push past but she was adamant about keeping them between her and our next step in the plan. They paused to look at her, and she must've said something that concerned them enough, to briefly take their eyes off of Dimitri. I ran over to the side of the parkade, I could see Sophia at, and surely, there came Elizabeth.

She subtly met Dimitri and pushed him in the direction of the alley. I saw them go into the back door and assumed they would make it okay. Sophia kept walking, going to another spot, I told her to sit and wait at. I didn't want all of them coming here, in case they were followed. They all had different pick-up points, for me to get them at, when this was all over.

I ran back down two flights of stairs, skipping most of them and sprinted to the side of the parkade, I told them Iwould be at. The meeting point. The moment I would get to see Dimitri again. I paced and paced, for what felt like enough time, for the earth to rotate one-hundred times.

Then it hit me. A wave of golden light, came onto my skin, making it tingle everywhere. I shivered, not with fear,

but with delight. I spun around and looked into the deep pits of love, right into Dimitri's eyes.

I flew over to him and wrapped my arms around him. Tears coming out of my eyes uncontrollably. I felt like I could fly and every pain I had ever felt, suddenly vanished. The hole in my heart was filled, and I no longer felt a void. I didn't feel like a stranger to this place anymore, I felt home.

I felt whole.

"Dimitri, oh my God. You're here," I cried, unable to pull my head away from being buried deep within his chest.

I took a deep inhale of his smell, and it hadn't changed one bit. Sandalwood, with a hint of juniper, the best smell in the world. I took another deep breath, basking in the glory that was Dimitri. And I felt a hand in my hair, then my bun was released from the pony tail, falling to my hips. He intertwined his fingers in it and then pulled back, to get a good look at me. I looked up to meet his eyes, with tears blocking my vision. Even in the blur, he looked perfect.

He cupped my face with his strong, yet delicate hands and wiped the tears from my cheeks.

"Emilia...You're alive. You're okay. Oh, God." He wept as he pulled me back into his chest. His hands gripped me, like I could be molded there and would never be able to leave again. I felt him kiss my head, then he leaned back, to kiss my forehead. As he did, I felt a teardrop hit me and looked up to see tears in his eyes, as well. I was stunned. I had never seen him cry before and it made him so... vulnerable, and so much more beautiful than ever.

He brought his face down to mine and met my lips, with a longing, I thought only I could possess for him. He kissed me, and the world felt like it vanished. It was only Dimitri and I that mattered anymore. I felt like we blended together, as two humans, with one soul. As he continued to kiss me, with such longing and passion, I too realized, he felt the same way.

We broke apart and just stared at each other, for a moment. Everywhere he touched, I felt a burning sensation. When I looked into his eyes, I saw his bright soul.

He was my match. My partner. My love.

"How did you know I would be here? And why go through all that trouble with the girls?" He asked me, while his hand played with a strand of my hair and the other stayed on my waist, keeping me close.

"Dimitri, I had to send them because it's not safe for us here. It isn't safe for me, or for you," I told him, with my hands around his neck. I took his hair out of the bun and started playing with it. I forgot how good-looking he was with it down. He truly looked like a Greek God.

"What do you mean? I've been all around, searching for you. We thought something bad happened. I was taken away on assignment under strict orders, and asked to help the son of a man, who knew my aunt. I got a message the next day that you went missing, and immediately quit the mission, to come help find you." He dropped the piece of my hair and cupped the side of my face again. I leaned into his hand, and rested my cheek there, looking up into his eyes.

"After you left, I was attacked. Someone tried to throw me into a van, but I fought them off," I showed him a scar on my arm, to emphasize how hard I had to fight these attackers.

"When that happened, I knew I had to leave town. I've been all over, putting the pieces together. Dimitri, we're not safe." And then I told him everything I had figured out since. I told him all about the animals, and the cabin. I told him about his aunt, and the men in suits. I even told him about Myles, and the conversation the Crow came to me with, back in Olympia.

After I finished, he just stared off, watching everything but seeing nothing. He held me close to him, and I knew his mind was somewhere else, possibly putting more pieces together. I wasn't sure if he would agree with me, but surely after all of the things we had been through, he would know. I also didn't know, if this would be a good time, to tell him I've been pregnant this entire time, but no time like the present, right?

"Dimitri…" I spoke, scared to break his concentration.

He looked down, with soft eyes and brushed some hair behind my ears.

"Yes, my love?" he asked with an affectionate tone. The one he would use when he knew I had been knocked down and just needed a little extra love that day.

"I, uh, am also, like, three months... pregnant. I think it's a boy. I've had dreams." I stumbled the words out at last and was anxious to hear what he would say. Would he be upset I was running around, trying to save him? Would he be mad, that I was pregnant at such a hectic time. Maybe I messed up... Why did I feel that way?

Instead, he did something I didn't expect. He dropped down to both knees, leaned into my body and started kissing my stomach, overtop of the overalls. His big hands, fit over most of my front abdominal area, especially with the way his fingers were all spread apart this time. He looked up at me, with more tears in his eyes, paired with such a radiant smile, it made me wonder why the sun even bothered to shine today. I knelt down to be eye level with him.

"I know this isn't a good time... but I had to tell you." I said in a quiet voice. I might've gotten down to be at eye level with him, but as I spoke, my eyes drifted to my hands as I nervously played with them.

"Emilia." He lifted my chin up, so I would meet him. Then he got up, grabbed my hand and lifted me to my feet in the process, "there is never, not a good time, to start a family with you. This is the happiest news I have ever received in my life. I love you so much matia mou."

When he used my nickname, I knew his heart was truly happy. In Greek it meant, My Moon. Since we met, I have always had a fascination with the moon and Dimitri had told me, I, too, shined on the darkness of his life like the moon did at night. We stood there, two happy, almost parents, on the run for their lives and it was truly magical.

I knew we were pressed for time, and the men would soon figure out where he had gone.

"We need to leave. Right now." I told him.

"Emilia, I can't just leave my aunt and never return. There are things that I need to take care of... If she is dirty, it's better for me to go back in, undercover and work the case from the inside. I can find out more," he said to me, as he looked around to make sure we still had some time.

"Are you out of your mind!? Dimitri, you cannot go back there. What are you thinking?" I was getting worked up but tried to keep my voice down. It was hard when your fiancé was being irrational.

"You're in danger and I can do something about it. That's it. I'm not going to let anything happen to you, or my son. Do you understand? Now that I am aware of the enemy, it'll be easier for me to take them out. No questions Emilia, and no eye rolls. This is who I am. I protect the ones I love. You of all people should understand this." He dropped his hands and brought them into a prayer at his chest. He was begging me to understand, and looking into his eyes I really did.

"Fine. But. I'm helping you," he began to protest and I put a hand over his mouth and used my free one to point and animate my rebuttal.

"Look, I'm just like you. I need to protect the ones I love and you know I can. Maybe I don't need to get my hands dirty, but I'm smart enough to be an asset. I got myself here, undetected. You taught me and here is your chance to see your work in action. No lip. I'm in. You can't stop me," I dropped my hands and waited for his reply.

I knew he was working this all out, in his detailed way of thinking. Always three steps ahead, and taking caution. He wouldn't have easily dismissed my protests, but I'm sure, knowing I was carrying his first child really threw him for a loop.

"Okay. But you take instructions from me. No side plans, Emilia, I'm serious. We pick a spot to meet every day and go over the information. It has to be different times, and locations every time. No phone calls and we limit the meetings to under twenty minutes. You do not come near Sylvia's house, at all. Period. No matter what message or vision any animal brings you. The minute something gets bad, you leave town and return to my family in Greece, they will know what to do if anything happens to me. Nothing can happen to you, and the baby. Do you understand?" I simply nodded.

Tears filled my eyes again and I really hated the entire world. I didn't even want to think about going on without Dimitri. He was right in front of me now, breathing and alive, but even the thought of him gone, made me sick to my stomach.

"I love you matia mou." He said as he pulled me in for a tight hug, and another passionate kiss.

We pulled away, knowing the seconds were ticking.

"Tomorrow, we meet at the bridge spot we first found when we moved here. Eight-fifteen in the morning. We will need your friends to be lookouts, so grab any electronic gear you can, her." He pulled out a bunch of hundred-dollar bills from his wallet. "take this, and be safe, Emilia. Oh,

God, please be safe." I knew we had to part ways. I took the money and as I did, he took my hand, and kissed it gently.

"What are you a drug dealer now, Dima? Carrying all that cash with you, it's unsafe really." I gave him a smile and he dropped my hand.

"See you tomorrow." He turned around and started to jog off.

"I love you," I whispered and just before he got too far, he turned around and blew me a kiss from the other end of the parkade.

I watched him go down the stairs but didn't dare look over the edge to see his departure. If those two men were around still, I didn't want to blow my cover. I stood there long enough, to allow the tears to stream down my face, like a waterfall crashing to the asphalt below me.

6. *Fight or Flight*

I looked at my watch and saw that it was pickup time. I jogged back to the stairs, running down to the Porsche
Elizabeth had given me the keys to. I just got in the car and just before I started it, I heard voices in the parkade.

"How dare you speak to me that way, Andrew!" I heard a female voice scream with anger. I hunched down in my seat but caught a glimpse in the rear-view mirror. A man and a woman were arguing by a truck directly behind the Porsche. They were standing only a few inches apart and I saw the man raise his hand to the woman, then he slapped her in the face.

"Don't you ever think you are equal to me. You are nothing, and never will be Janica," he said, as he went to building raise his hand again.

With no second thought, I was out of the car and on the move. I sprinted over just in time to catch him off guard and shove him so hard he flew into the back of the truck, with a loud thud. I immediately put myself in a protective stance, between him and the woman he called, Janica.

There was no way I was going to let him touch her again.

"Who the hell are you?" He screamed, coming toward me. He quickly came at me and caught me in the left side of the face with a punch. I took the hit because I saw his form and knew it was sloppy. The harder he threw his hand, the harder he would fall. At the end of the hit, I had no feeling, only pure adrenaline. I grabbed his arm and pulled it towards me, while kicking him straight in the stomach, disconnecting his shoulder. He screamed in agony and started to cuss at me. I backed up, with the woman behind me.

"I'll take you where you need to go, or you can stay. Your call, but I'm leaving," I told her as we moved closer to the Porsche. I dared a look behind me, and saw that she was terrified. The look on her face was like she had just seen a ghost. She moved her eyes from the man to me and gave me a quick nod.

We got into the Porsche, and sped away. I had never driven so fast in my life. I had to pick up the others at the meeting spot and it only took me six minutes to get there, rather than fifteen. They gave me questioning looks, as I motioned for them to get into the backseat but none of us said a word.

I decided it would be a good idea, for all of us to eat and calm down, from the job we just did, so I pulled into a roadside food truck picnic area. I ordered everyone something good enough, and we all sat down to wait for it come out.

"Emilia, what happened to your face?" asked Sophia, always brave enough to ask the things no one else wanted to.

"She saved me," said the woman from the parkade, Janica. It was barely audible but we all heard. They looked at her strangely, but she met their eyes with fierceness.

"How?" said Sophia.

"My ex-husband was going to beat me, like usual." She started to sob, but kept pushing to explain, "I have been trying to stand up to him for years, and today I tried, but he hit me. Thank God your friend was there, because she came in and saved me before it could get worse."

"What's your name?" asked Victoria with a look of compassion on her face, I recognized from the nights when
I needed extra love.

"I'm Janica Frosher."

"I'm Victoria Johnson and this is my daughter, Sophia, and my sister Elizabeth. And this, is Emilia Diomades. Her nickname, is The Warrior," she added with a wink.

"It's nice to meet you all, thank you for your help today. I really don't want to be a burden on you, but I needed to get out of there," Janica said to me, and I heard a trace of a Jamaican accent.

There were tears rolling down her beautiful brown cheeks. They held a hue of pink, that would've put the blush industry to shame. She was nervous and ran her hand through her beautifully curled afro, that was styled perfectly to shape her face. She was so beautiful, and it hurt me to think, that anyone would be nothing but loving towards her.

"It's not your fault. Please don't blame yourself, I'm happy to help. If you need a place to stay, you can crash at our place." I told her as I grabbed her hand and gave her a warm smile. She met my gaze, and nodded again.

The waitress came, breaking our moment, but relieving us of our hunger. We ate, and made our way back to the house.

Janica's response to the mansion was that of mine as well. She was astonished at the beauty and was happy to have her own room. Victoria gave her some pyjama's and she went right to bed. It hurt me to see women torn down so much, by outside forces. My heart hurt for all of them.

"Get ice on your eye, or it'll be real ugly tomorrow," Victoria told me, as we headed to the kitchen to get some tea before bed. Sophia joined us and we sat at the island.

"What happened with Dimitri today?" Sophia inquired with an eye brow raise.

Just like always, I got a dreamy look on my face as I replayed the events and the magnitude of our reconnecting. I told them how beautiful it was, and how excited he is to have a baby. I also let them know that they would be meeting him tomorrow.

"What are we going to do about Janica?" Victoria asked.

"We can leave her here with Elizabeth. I think I'll only need you two tomorrow, and she could use the company." I told them both. They agreed and then headed off to bed.

I was too keyed up to sleep just yet, so I went to sit outside by the pool. I took one of the sage green throws, off the couch near the patio door and wrapped it around me. I went out and sat in the patio chair with my tea, to watch the water dance, with the moonlight. It was close to being a half moon, but not quite yet. I knew this was the time that energy was shifting on the planet. More and more came from the moon and I could feel it rushing through my veins.

I sat there and let all the events play out in my mind. I knew this all had to happen, I just wish it wasn't my life. We get what we can handle, but really, I was tired of handling so much at once. It felt like I was going to explode at any moment of the day, and I hated it. I tried to keep it together, for the sake of the people around me, but what I really wanted to do, was change lives.

If Dimitri's aunt was trying to eradicate witches, if men stopped seeing woman as beneath them, and if people treated everyone equally this world would be a much better place.

I sat for a good amount of time thinking about a new earth, and then I knew it was time for some rest. Dimitri would be very interested in knowing where I got the black eye from, so on my way up to bed, I grabbed an ice pack to try and lessen the severity of the bruise.

The bridge hadn't changed one bit in the time I had been away from it. I knew where to go, and felt nostalgic, at how easy life seemed so long ago. Or was it long ago at all?

I didn't understand time anymore.

"Here, take these," I said to Victoria and Sophia as I handed them walkie-talkies and ear pieces. They set them up and we all got on the same channel.

"These are really cool. I feel like a spy," remarked Sophia.

"Me too, Sof. Dimitri told me to get them, so I bought them this morning while you were still sleeping. They go by satellite but have an encryption, so we can communicate anywhere, non-detected." I said with a grin. I felt like a little kid playing cops and robbers.

"So cool," she gasped as she played with it.

"Can we go through the plan one more time? I just want to make sure I understand," Victoria asked me, looking a little more anxious today than yesterday. Apparently sitting down was harder than throwing trash cans for her. I loved the intensity she brought.

"I have to meet Dimitri in a certain spot under the bridge. I need you two to stand fairly close to the centre, and watch for anything suspicious. People looking attentive, men dressed in suits, someone who also has an ear-piece. Anything that seems a little off, radio us. I'm giving Dimitri one, so he'll be in the loop."

They both nodded and headed off. It was eight-fourteen and I jogged over to our spot. If I was a minute late, so help me, God. I knew punctuality was a big thing for Dimitri and it was the only characteristic that I loathed about him. I got to the rock formation, just as my watch beeped, indicating it was time for the meeting.

Dimitri came out of no where, and halted right in front of me, making me jump a little.

"Dima, what the hell! Are you trying to give me a heart attack!?" I exclaimed as I put my hand over my chest.

"I'm just making you better, that's all matia mou." He said as he touched my face and pulled me into a kiss.

"What happened to your eye?"

"Oh, uh... nothing." I said as I shrugged it off.

"No. What happened? Who did it?" He asked, in a 'don't bullshit me' way.

"Just some guy in a parkade. He was hitting a woman, and I got out to defend her. Don't worry though, I dislocated his shoulder." I said with a wink.

"Emilia." His tone indicated he believed it was no joking matter.

"What? Was I just supposed to let her get beat right behind me, Dimitri? You off all people understand how important it is to me to stand up for domestic abuse! Was I supposed to drive away, knowing I could've helped?" I started to lose my temper.

He went to grab my hand but I was so mad, I pulled away from him. There was no way, I was going to let him tell me I was wrong, for what I did. Maybe other times when I let my impulses get the best of me, I understood. But this wasn't that time, and I was no longer a teenage girl.

"Emilia, you did the right thing. But, you aren't just fighting with your body right now. You're fighting with a baby growing inside of you. Be careful. Don't take silly risks," he said in a soothing voice.

I knew then, that he just meant the best. I relaxed a little and rested my head on his chest. He stroked my hair, and to my amazement, I felt a tingle of energy rush through me, unlike the usual burning, I got from his touch. This wasn't anything to do with how I felt about him, but rather a transfer of energy.

"Did you just try to heal me?" I said, pulling back to study him. I was shocked.

"Try? I succeeded. Your eye is less bruised." He tucked some hair behind my ear, and I began to blush. "I've been practicing what you taught me."

"Wow, you're amazing." I got on my tip-toes and gave him a kiss that sent a fire through my entire body. I jumped on him and continued that passion through my every touch.

"Emilia, we're on a mission…" He whispered in my ear and it took every ounce of strength I had, to calm down. It was so hard to keep our clothes on, when we were together, but I knew he was right about today.

I let out a huge groan, and stood back on the ground again.

"Okay, let's get down to business then. Tell me what you learned," I told him.

"You were right about Sylvia. She's very adamant about finding you and having you 'dealt with'," he told me in a matter of fact tone, keeping it professional without emotion. I didn't understand how he could speak about my impending death so easily. Me? I felt like I was just barely keeping it together.

"So, what do we do from here?" I asked. There had to be a plan.

"Well, there are a lot of logistics we can go through, but I know you've never been a fan of that. To keep it simple, we have to deal with her and the Anova's, before they find you."

"And how are we going to do that? We don't know where they are, how many there are, or even what they look like!" I exclaimed feeling more and more of the pressure upon me. It felt like the world was closing in on me and I could no longer escape.

"With me. I work from the inside, like I told you yesterday. You and your friends work from the outside. I called Donny, and Luca. They're on their way. They'll be set up just outside of town, and will come in to help me and you, if you need it. We'll get through this my love, I promise."

"Donny and Luca are coming? Wow. This could turn ugly." I looked at the ground and began kicking the dirt with my feet.

Those two didn't come to just have fun, they came to take care of business. I thought Dimitri was the deadliest guy I knew but he didn't even hold a candle light next to the Ratnikov brothers. Donny and Luca were born in

Greece, but moved to Moscow, Russia, when they were little. They served in the military and had other ties to the underground, not-so-legal armies.

Dimitri only knew them from past government operations, when he went to Russia to help out. Dimitri had saved their lives, more times than anyone could count, so they were in debt to him for life.

The scariest thing about these brothers was the ruthlessness they carried. When Dimitri fought, he did it with honour and integrity. Luca and Donny fought because they liked it.

"It's going to be fine. With all of us together, there isn't anyone that can stop us. Emilia, look at me." He gave me a gentle touch on the chin to lift my face. "No one on this earth is going to touch you, do you understand me? I'll die a thousand deaths, before I let anything happen to you."

I looked up to meet his eyes, and saw the fire behind them. Other people didn't know what to do with all the passion he held, but me? I did. I knew he was serious. He wouldn't let anything harm me, even if it meant he himself died in the process. I might look wild and untamed, but Dimitri was just the same. He hid it behind a mask, but I knew.

"Thank you, Dimitri." was all I could say.

He told me some instructions, and I listened to every word. In detail, he went over the days plan for him and told me where we could meet tomorrow evening. It was a spot he and I had been to once, but no where we visited frequently. He wanted to keep us undetected and not form a pattern for anyone to understand. His training was impeccable.

"Okay," I told him after he told me the plan for the tenth time, "I get it Dima. I don't get to do anything super fun. I just have to watch the area and ask the animals to spy. It's a lot of magic, you know. Someone else who uses, or feels it will be able to find me."

"Isn't there a way you could use a protection prayer or something along those lines?" He asked.

I hadn't ever told him I could channel my ancestors. The things they told me are private and close to my heart. I felt like that was a special thing I kept just for me to know. He was right though, Elayo would know how to protect my spirit from other magic users.

"I can try to charm some jewelry, but I'll have to go buy some silver. Can I have some money?" I asked. I had my own money, but my cash supply was dwindling. If I had access to say my bank account, then it would be no problem.

He went into his pocket and pulled his wallet out. He had two times the amount of cash he had yesterday and I was seriously concerned with how much he was carrying around. He handed me, what looked like a couple thousand in hundreds and I was stunned.

"Relax, Emilia. I like cash over plastic." He gave me a devil-may-care smile, and I again felt like I couldn't allow him to be clothed for much longer.

"You need to go. I want to rip your clothes off right here and now. But we're on a mission and your sexiness is compromising it." I sounded like a crazy girl but I didn't care. He was sexy and I wanted him. He needed to know.

"You make it hard for a man to walk away, but you're right. We're just over fifteen minutes, and we need to leave."

He pressed the button on the radio, "Are we clear up there? No spectators?"

I heard Sophia's voice in my ear piece, "We're clear. Over." I chuckled a bit and Dimitri looked at me strangely.

"I met her in a high school four days ago and now we're spies, saying 'over' through a radio with ear pieces. I need to laugh because this is unreal."

He smiled and gave me a tight hug. He kissed my forehead, and then brought his lips down to mine for a quick, sweet kiss. Obviously avoiding the possible mess, we could get ourselves into, if we let our guards down. He knelt down and kissed my tiny baby bump.

"I love you," he whispered, and then met my eyes. He held them for a moment longer, and then turned to walk away. I watched, feeling like the world was a cruel and unfair place. I waited a couple of minutes and then set up the hill, to where the others waited for me.

When I got to the middle of the bridge, Sophia and Victoria we're sitting there, looking very professional.

"You guys look like you could do this for a living, you know." I joked as I walked up to stand by them.

They chuckled.

"No way, too intense for me." Victoria shook her head and I could see how tense she was here.

"I could do it, I like this spy mission. I think it's so fun."

Sophia spoke cheerfully. I think at this point, she would like anything with excitement.

We stood at the bridge's railing for a bit, staring off at the river that flowed through the city.

"Time to go?" I asked.

"Yes, let's go." Victoria replied.

7. Alone

A lot of the next few days looked the same. I met with Dimitri periodically, and he told me the information he learned from the inside. I sent animal guides to help him, and to seek more answers. The other women helped me with whatever tasks I needed, but I often just gave them lookout positions and then told them to go out and still enjoy the time they had.

Victoria ended up extending their vacation, which meant Sophia didn't have to go to school, for another week or so. Apparently, she was an honour student already, so the time away, wasn't really going to affect her all that much. Janica decided to stay with us, as she arranged for her things to be packed up by her other family members and brought to a house that didn't involve abuse.

She was planning on moving in with her younger brother, which she didn't like, but it was better than any other option.

"So, Andrew is your ex-husband but you were still living together?" I asked as we sat in the living room one morning, drinking tea. I didn't need to meet Dimitri today, to keep things more low-key. He just asked me, to still send animals, and ask questions.

"Yeah, it was a weird situation. I didn't have anywhere else to go at the time of our divorce. I gave up my career for him. He just let me live off of his money, but as soon as I wanted to go on my own, he cut me off, keeping me there."

Janica explained with pain written all over her face.

"I'm sorry he was so abusive. That isn't easy to go through," I leaned over to touch her hand and send her some healing. She didn't seem as nervous or as fragile, as she did the day I met her in the parkade. It seemed over the last few days, she really grew into herself. Being around good people, must've helped her develop.

I noticed more and more of her features today, moving my eyes across her, with a gentle smile on my face. She had very beautiful light brown eyes with a hint of amber to them. They looked like they had seen too much, and held sadness in them. Her hair was braided today, and went down to her middle back. I noticed a tattoo on her ribs as she was in a sports bra and shorts, something she had borrowed from Elizabeth. I ~~would've~~ never have thought Elizabeth, to have a sports bra handy, but hey, I guess that teaches me to not assume. I had a good feeling about her as a person.

I pulled back my hand and knew some of my healing worked, just by the change in her aura. Sometimes I healed people without them knowing, but it was always much more effective, when the subject wanted the healing done.

However, I couldn't help myself, but to give light.

"You and Elizabeth are really getting along, eh? It's nice to see." I asked.

"Yeah, she's really great. She's so beautiful and she doesn't even see it. I really enjoy spending time with her. She makes me feel safe." She spoke with a certain fondness, I only heard when people were in love. I was a bit confused, but let it go.

"Yes, she is great. You two, are great together." And I meant what I said. Seeing them together was really nice. On the outside it appeared that they were opposite of each other. Elizabeth had straight bleach blonde hair, fair skin with the slightest amount of a pink undertone paired with jade green eyes. But on the inside, they had a lot in common.

They had both been abused by their partners, and were seeking to rebuild. Elizabeth was still married, but I had a feeling that being away from her husband and around so much love was really helping her growth. They seemed to be on the same path.

"It's time I go for a walk in the woods, I will be back soon. Will you tell the others, I've gone to 'talk with the trees'?" I said, as I stood up to leave.

"Sure. Be safe out there," she said with genuine concern in her eyes.

I nodded and took my leave.

I found it odd, to have people know about what I could do. It was a thing I had kept hidden, for so long, because I wasn't sure what people would do to me. Would they accept me? Would they exile me? Use me for my talents? Or simply burn me at the stake, like they did all my ancestors?

It was hardly a fate I wanted to face, but somehow it ended up becoming a mountain, I needed to overcome.

I stepped away from the mansion, and into the forest.

Today was about me, and connecting with my spirit. I found a perfect spot beside the river, along the tree line. The sun reflected a beautiful shimmering light off the water and I took a deep breath, grateful to be in the presence of such beauty. I sat on some grass I had found, and smelled the blooming flowers.

"Coltsfoot, how nice it is to see you up already. Thank you," I spoke softly, showing love to the wildflower. I sighed. I completely lost track of time. Suddenly, a noise in the trees brought me back to the present. I looked to where it was coming from and saw a crow, on top of a pine tree.

"Do you have something for me?" I asked aloud.

Yes. Watch out.

Immediately I felt a sick twist within the pits of my stomach. I looked around seeing no one, but I couldn't shake the feeling of the goosebumps, all over me. I grabbed the closest thing to a weapon – a giant rock – and ran back up the hill towards the house.

As I ran, I heard the birds fly out of the trees, away from the house my friends were at. I ran harder.

When I finally broke out of the trees, I was relieved to see the house untouched.

"Holy...." was all I could say.

"Ahhh!" I screamed aloud as someone grabbed me and dragged me back into the trees.

"No! Stop!" I yelled at the top of my lungs. Hoping anyone would hear. The person put their hand over my mouth, and I fought hard to shake them off.

"The harder you fight, the worse it'll be, Emilia." A snake like voice hissed at me. Whoever this was, I already hated him. I elbowed him in the stomach, but he didn't budge. "Fine. Do it the hard way."

Something hit me in the back of the head, and I fell to the ground. Barely conscious, I looked up to see who it was. The man that looked like death, with the scar on his face knelt down and covered my head with a black bag.

My eyes fluttered, as I tried to wake up to whatever hell I was in. My eyelids felt like sandbags, and I ached to keep them open. Finally, as I was able to take in my sights, I felt a sharp pain in the back of my head. I reached back to feel it, and sure enough, there was a giant lump.

"Ow," I whispered as I dug through my hair to find any other injuries. I quickly brought my hands to my belly, and was relieved to see no harm was done. Dragging my eyes up from the ground, to take in more of my surroundings, I was shocked to see the things my eyes had laid upon. I was in no place, like this world. I sat in a cave. But not just any cave, the kind that looked like it was used as a dungeon before.

Cobwebs hung in the corners, and scratch marks, from nails lined the walls. I peered around to find the only light source, coming in from a part of the wall which held a torch. I felt this cold, eerie-ness to this place, and didn't dare let my guard down. I didn't want to feel this place out. I didn't want to know what lay ahead of me. I looked down, to see what was going on with my feet, that felt incredibly heavy and realized I was chained to the wall by hard steel. The only indication of age on them, was a little rust, along the part that held my ankle, but otherwise looked like it could keep someone in here, for a very long time.

Panic shot through me, as I tried to think of what happened. I was stuck in a cave. Not just any cave, but a cave that looked like death, was dealt here more often than not. My hands were free, so I tried my hardest to pull the chains from the stone wall. When that failed, I tried to pry them off of my feet, which only resulted in damaging the skin and making myself bleed.

Thankfully, my attackers left me in my jeans, and sweatshirt, but took my shoes along with everything else, I had on me. The only piece of jewelry left, was a silver earring in my cartilage on my left ear. Thankfully, it was a healing charm I made with Elayo's advice, a long time ago. I fought for a little while longer, against the harsh conditions, I found myself in. My feet were dirty from the dirt floor, and my body was exhausted from losing this match.

I eventually came to a seated position against the wall, and started to sob. I ran my hands along my face and wondered what I must've done to deserve this.

I heard footsteps and immediately sprang up, shaking my fear away and readied for an attack.

"Well, Miss.Diomades, so good to see you're awake." Sylvia stepped into the cave. At first, it was hard to make her out, with the little light source coming in, but as she strode closer to the fire, I could see her clearly. She had an old face, that looked like death, as well. Her eyes were cunning, and if they were a colour, I could hardly make it out, as they looked as if they were all pupil. Her thin, greying hair, didn't help her much either. She was in her sixties - or so, I thought. Today, she wore a red sundress, with fur over top of it. The fur made me flinch. She didn't deserve to wear an animal. I had never noticed before, but I really did hate her. I could see her act, clearly now.

"Wish I could say the same for you." Venom hung in the air from my words, and I was taken aback by how harsh my voice sounded.

She gave me a harsh snarl, "be quiet girl, you have no idea what you're talking about. I'm here to simply free you of this miserable state. Being a witch is not natural. You're an abomination. A creation that shouldn't be allowed to walk. I am only doing my nephew, and the rest of the world a favour. Your sister didn't seem to mind..." She snapped, and then her face turned into a smirk as she brought up my sister.

"Wh-what did you say, about my sister?" I asked through gritted teeth. Surely, I was going to black out. All I could see was red, tinging my vision, and my blood boiling to extreme levels.

"Never mind her. We're here for you. Now, you have two choices. One, I kill you, and you die." she shrugged, "or you can become one of us, and give up your soul. There are perks to the second one. You will never die. You will continuously take victims, and transfer into their bodies. One day you will look like this," she gestured to me up and down, "and the next you can look like a super-model," she smiled.

I didn't say anything. I just stared, mouth open. It took me a few more moments, then I would've liked to formulate, enough words to speak.

"Give up my soul? Then what would I be? I would be living an empty life. Like you." I stumbled the words out, still shocked that, that, was even a thing.

"Yes, well, I would prefer that. You have quite the powerful soul. I can't risk it coming back, or being allowed on this earth, I'm sure you can understand. But, if you get annoying, I will not hesitate to kill you now, and then plan, the hunt for you in your next life." She came closer to me, her cunning eyes making me feel more nauseous than I have ever been.

"I won't give up my soul you crazy bitch!" I snarled at her, pulling as fast as I could, from the cave wall.

"I guess, you just need some more time to think then." She smiled, then turned around and walked towards the exit. She shot a glance back at me, and before she left me here, she said, "I'm sure you'll change your mind once we've starved and tortured you enough." Then with that, I was alone in my own personal hell.

I didn't see anyone, for a couple days, after my initial abduction. I kept playing all the details in my head, about what was really going on. Was I truly going to die here? Or were they going to steal my soul? How does my sister fit into all this? Is the baby, going to be, okay? Why was Sylvia so obsessed with her 'nephew' if she has been alive, for so many years? Would that really be her nephew then? On and on it went. I tried to think of anything else, but my mind was racing and my body was weak.

After a while of pacing, I sat down in the corner, I now made my safe zone. It wasn't that safe, but it was the only place, in the cave, that I dug out a place to sleep. I tried to summon a spirit guide, or an animal but I kept getting blocked. It was like something was interfering with my antenna...

I blanked out completely and decided to try again.

Maybe all I needed was to calm down... I was over-working, and hungry after all, so maybe, just maybe it was me...

A sound in the cave startled me, and I opened my eyes, to stare into the darkness, with a man before me. Scar face, with his evil eyes looked right into mine, a couple of inches from my face and began to smile that awful smile, each insane person was wearing around here, lately. Did it come, in the cult manual or something?

"You will never be able to touch the magic here, little girl, stop trying. You're making a fool of yourself." His snake like voice hissed out at me, as he rose from crouching close to my corner.

"Who the hell are you?" I snapped, as I began to stand up. I stumbled a bit from the loss of food and water, but tried hard to not look weak.

"Haven't you heard? I'm justice." He said, sweeping his arms over a bag filled with stuff, I couldn't see from where I was.

"I don't think you're doing a very good job, at being anything but a psychopath." I said sternly, as I crossed my arms over my chest, in a defensive maneuver. This was the same man I had seen in each vision, but where the hell had I seen him, from before? This was so annoying, I needed to get down to the bottom of it.

Maybe he could fill me in, on where Dimitri was, as well...

"Tough talk from a weak girl chained to stone, no?" He began to shift things around in his mystery bag, and I started to feel sick again. Not because of the baby, but because of the fate that awaited me. He pulled out a stone. It was red, and looked like lava was held inside of it. It looked like what I thought the 'catholic of hell' would look like, and I suddenly began backing away. I hit a wall, and began to mentally chastise myself for being an idiot. Obviously, I couldn't get very far.

"Ahhhh, the great Emilia has been silenced." He stepped closer, and I felt cold all over. His vibe was disgusting, and made me feel like I was in the exorcism movies. He came to stand right in front of me and looked in my eyes.

"Hold this." He commanded as he held out the stone. I hesitated and kept my hands over my stomach.

He looked at me impatiently. "Word has it, that your boyfriend is out looking for you with one of my men. If you don't do as I say, I'll have my man snap your boyfriends pretty like neck, like that." He emphasized his words with a snap of his finger, to really drive his point across.

Only a few thoughts passed through my mind, but none were coherent. Surely, no one could Kill Dimitri... He was so good at fighting, so smart and always ahead of the game. He couldn't kill him, could he?

I decided I wouldn't chance his life. I held out my hands and he placed the stone in them. It was small, like a baseball, but shaped like an egg. I had this weird sensation flow through me, and all of a sudden, my blood began to boil. Not just normal boil, like when I got angry, but boil as in I began to sweat, and scream, as this pain shot through, every part of my body. I dropped the stone, but the feeling didn't go away. I screamed and screamed, as I thought I was going to explode from the agony. I dropped down to my hands and knees, just as the man began to laugh.

His laugh, sent chills down my spine. I felt disgusted, at the thought of laughing at someone in pain, never mind creating that pain and then laughing. Is that what it was like, to be soulless? I would never allow myself, to become that way, ever. I determined, right in my most painful moment, that I would rather die. I lifted my head enough for him to see the look in my eyes.

"Nice try, but you'll have to kill me," I spoke through gritted teeth, and spat on the ground, to really drive my point across.

The man knelt down beside me, grabbed my neck, and jerked me up off the ground.

"This is just the beginning my dear," he let my neck go, and walked away, leaving me breathless.

I laid down on the ground and began to cry. I cried so much, I began to doze off. For the first time in two days, I allowed myself to give into the exhaustion.

I felt a sensation of a dream coming on. It was foggy, but I was conscious enough in it that I could make it out. I could see I was in a field, full of blood and all around me was fog, and nothing more. I couldn't see beyond it, but I knew standing here was a bad idea. At one point I heard Elayo's voice, speak to me. "It isn't over, get up Emilia. You have to fight. You have to try! Ichbar et tu ichbar... Emilia get up! Fight! You will make it through this!"

I woke, startled.

I looked around the cave and saw that nothing had changed. I was still chained to the wall, starving and dreaming of water. Elayo's word stuck in my mind, but I was basically hopeless at this point. There was nothing around me, except for the painful ball of lava, Scarface made me hold yesterday. It glowed like the eyes of Satan, and I made sure I stayed far away from it. I briefly thought about what Dimitri would do. I hadn't had much time to process this situation, never mind think of him. I was already in too much pain, I didn't want to inflict any more on myself. But, this time, I would allow myself to think about him. Yes... What would he do? How would he react? What had he also told me to do, when I was in trouble?

"Emilia. What happens if you're in the wilderness with nothing to eat or drink? How will you survive, how will you defend yourself?" He asked me, with a stern look on his face. Those were the kinds of looks I was intimidated by.

"I'll talk to the Earth, and ask her for help Dima. I'll dance with the animals, and speak to the moon. I'll find my way home... Mother Earth would never let me down." I said in a joking matter, to take the edge off the conversation we were having, on a summer night in Athens.

"Let's say you don't have access to that– no wait–-" He held up a hand, to silence my protest, "what if you can't access those powers? What will you do?" He grilled me for the next hour, as we walked through the ancient ruins.

The flickering of fire, brought my attention to the only light source in the cave. Somewhere, in the back of my mind, an idea started to tickle. The fire... The flames danced and danced, like they were being sculpted, by the air alone. Fire. An element. I wonder if it could work. My thinking was abruptly cut off, when Sylvia entered the cave, with her henchmen, Scarface and the other suit guy.

"Oh look, the three musketeers. To what do I owe the honour?" I asked as I began to rise from the floor. I threw enough sass in there to get dirty looks from my captors.

"We've come to see if you will join us," Sylvia spoke, as she walked closer to me, leaving the two men further back.

Today, she wore all black, and tied her thin greying hair up in a ponytail.

"If you can take any body you want, why do you keep this old one? It's clear it's weak." I asked, crossing my arms over my chest.

"Excellent question. I keep it, because I need my nephew to trust me a little longer. I'm sure stealing another body won't be okay, for that self righteous brat," she remarked.

I scoffed. How dare she talk about the love of my life, like he was anything but the best man in this entire universe.

"And anyways, it can't be any weaker than yours." She started to pace in front of me, and I had to remind myself that three against one wasn't very good odds, if I tried to strangle her right now.

"Well, I certainly won't be joining you. Please just kill me, and be on your way. The dust you're stirring up, is quite annoying and I would like it all to be over soon." I said to her, watching her every move. Sizing her up.

"Unlikely." She stopped and turned towards me. "Jeff and John, aren't the type to let someone off, with an easy death."

She beckoned them towards me.

"Emilia, pleasant seeing you here." Scarface, who apparently has a name as boring as John, spoke to me with his snake like voice. I rolled my eyes.

"I've instructed Jeff and John, to take measures into their own hands if you do not have a decision by tonight. If I have it my way, your soul will leave this earth and your immortality will stay here to serve me forever." She smiled and they all turned to leave.

"Drop dead," I murmured under my breath, and to my amazement, they all laughed as they walked out. I wonder, if becoming an Anova, meant you incurred super hearing.

The encounter went through my mind, for the next hour. I mulled her words over and over in my mind. I kept thinking about what it would be like to be one of those evil people. So cruel and calculating. No sparkle to my eyes, just hard, and soulless. Plus, I would never be able to touch the earth, in the same way, as I could now.

I thought about what life would be like, if I wasn't able to feel nature the way I did. What if I didn't understand that everything is connected to everything else? That we were all, part of the same, intelligent consciousness? I couldn't process, not being able to see a soul behind the eyes of every animal. And the healing? Oh, I couldn't give that up.

That was part of my mission here on earth. I needed to heal it. I needed to love. I had to be alive, and I had to be free. No. I would never give up my soul, and I wouldn't be dying here either.

There was no way, I was going to leave this beautiful place. No way I was going to let my family down. I was not going to leave Dimitri. And I sure as hell wasn't going to let anything happen to my son!

For the hundredth time today, I took a deep breath and stood up, straight. Determination, running through my veins, like cars driving too fast, on the freeway. I felt goosebumps all over, and I finally understood what it meant to get up ten. I quickly rationalized everything I could. I looked at this cave through different eyes now, eyes that weren't afraid.

Eyes that wouldn't back down.

8. Inner Power

I took in every detail of the cave, and made some mental notes. I knew there were some loose rocks in parts, I couldn't quite reach. I saw everything in a new perceptive and remembered who I was. I went over to the hell stone, filled with lava that no one bothered to take. I looked it over, and hit it with the chain around my feet. It glowed, and affected the chains very little. They heated slightly and then the heat went away.

Okay. So, the lava rock heats, when it comes into contact with anything, not just human skin. I thought it was weird, that John held it and felt nothing, but stored that in my mind for later.

What was that saying, about fighting fire with fire? I thought back to everything I learned in chemistry, over the years. Metal had a boiling point. It was hotter than anything, a human could endure...

But wait! I had a healing charm, still in my ear.

I decided that my insanity, had officially left the building, and now I had to act, before my time was up. I quickly took the earring out of my ear, and placed it into my hands. "Ichbar e tu ichbar." I hummed and I rocked back and forth, hoping the protection mantra worked with the tiny bit of silver I had. I slid the earring onto my pinky finger, and didn't feel much of a difference. I wasn't sure if that was what was supposed to happen, but decided to chance it.

With all of the strength I had, after starving, for the last three days, I picked up that stupid little stone, and threw it as hard as I could, at the cave wall. Nothing happened except the heat in my hands flared up, and the rock bounced back to me.

"You little son of a b---" I gasped, as the rock flared up at me speaking to it. Did this thing have a mind?

"Okay. I need you to explode when you hit the wall of the cave." It flared up and I took that as a sign.

I picked it up and threw it hard against the stone wall. Nothing happened, except this time, it didn't burn my hands, it just bounced back to me. A dead end.

No. There must be a way. The fire from the torch, caught my attention. What if I threw the stone into the fire?

"Okay, worth a shot. When I throw you into the fire, explode, and then heat the walls of the cave so much, that my chains turn into liquid, okay?" It glowed, and I decided it was my last shot.

I threw that stone – which apparently wasn't so stupid after all – into the fire and BOOM.

Fire went everywhere. It spilled all over from the torch, and came rapidly towards me. Part of it touched the wall, and went along the cave. It first covered only the part by the torch, then soon ran along the walls in all directions.

Everything glowed a beautiful orange, and I felt a rush of heat, from the excitement and beauty.

Eventually, the orange light reached my chains, and started climbing all the way up to my feet. I felt the heat on them, but it was nothing I couldn't handle. Then, the message from the stone, must've kicked it because the chains started to change into a bright, bright orange.

They were so bright I couldn't even look at them, and my feet? Oh, they were practically on fire. I could smell my skin burning and was on the verge of passing out.

Move! I heard a command and moved quickly. My feet were free and the melted metal, lay in a pool.

"Oh my God…" I breathed. I couldn't believe it. I could wield all sorts of magic, but this, I would've never thought myself capable of. I quickly touched my ankles to assess the damage, and saw there were at least second-degree burns.

No time to dwell on that yet. My adrenaline could carry me through a get away – if I could even find out where I was. I ran over to the mystery bag, John carried in, to see what I could use.

The amount of fire in the cave was so bright, it was like day time. I ran my hands over some of the things and didn't like what I saw. A lot of weapons, and more stones, that looked just as magical as this one had. For people who said they hated witches, I wasn't so sure they did.

I saw a knife, and some gloves. I took them along with a tarp, rope and this stone that looked like the galaxy was inside of it. I didn't know what it did, but it looked cool and something told me I might need it.

I could hardly run with all of these things in my hands, so I dumped the bag out onto the floor, and stuffed the things I wanted back inside. I made it into a backpack, but kept the knife out. Next thing I knew, I was assessing my escape. I didn't know where I was, but Sylvia's words, made it seem like it was daytime outside. I didn't want to take the torch with me, so I could go undetected, but I didn't know how long this cave went on for.

I looked over the bag of contents one more time, and saw a lighter. I decided that would have to work.

I began walking through the cave and let the light guide me, until I could just barley see. I came to a standstill, with two exits. One on the left, and one on the right. I felt more uncertain than I ever have in my life, but chose to go right.

I walked, stumbling only sometimes when there was a rock. I tried to be as quiet as possible, but everywhere I turned it was black. I decided to use my hands to guide me. The cold stone interior kept me alert, and felt nice on my skin, after having my ankles practically melted off.

I saw a patch of light coming in through a crack and headed towards it. Once I got there, I realized there was a boulder sealing the exit, to what looked like more mountain. I wouldn't be able to fit through it, but I could possibly try to move the boulder.

I used all my strength to try and push it, but it didn't move. I tried again, and again but nothing happened. I felt like giving up, but then I heard footsteps from the outside, coming towards me. I quickly ducked into a slit in the wall, and watched.

The boulder moved and let in a wave of light. Beautiful golden sunlight, I was so happy to see it, after all this time, it gave me more hope than what I had two minutes ago.

Jeff stepped through the entryway, holding yet another mystery bag. What was up with these psychopaths? I thought about what I could do, but then I realized, he was about to close the entryway back up, with the boulder, and I just couldn't let that happen. I had two seconds of a surprise attack, and I wasn't going to let it go.

I leaped out, striking him hard, into the side of the cave. He hit his head but quickly recovered. He was much taller than me, and much stronger. He wore the same suit I had always seen him in, and a look of pure hatred all over his face. He came in with an attack move and struck out, to land a blow to the side of my head. It shook me but I wasn't going to let that slow me down. Men always thought women were beneath them, when it came to anything physical, but that always left room for us to surprise them.

I moved fast, and we circled each other, waiting for the other to attack.

"There's no way you're getting out of here now, princess." Jeff spoke, voice cold and clearly agitated.

"How did you guys even find me in the first place?" I asked, keeping my guard up, but still curious as to how this all even happened.

"It was easy, once we knew you were back. Your man is too smart to catch off guard, but your friends? They are hardly, the mastermind's, they think they are. We spotted the Porsche leaving the same area Dimitri had been spotted in." He sounded more smug, than ever.

"Then you just decided to grab me, and think no one would notice?" I dodged a kick from him, and snaked one out myself that landed a soft blow to his knee. It was quite the dance.

"No. We knew they would notice. We've been watching them. After you're no longer a threat, we will dispose of them." He shrugged and sent a jab, that connected with my shoulder. I was in serious danger of passing out, but my defensive traits kicked in and I knew I needed to get back to my friends.

I faked him out, pretending to jab with my left, and while he was distracted, I got him in the side of the head with a hook. He stumbled, and I used to momentum to shove him into the side of the cave, hard enough that he hit his head again. We grappled, and he shoved me to the ground.

We fought there for a bit, as he tried to pin my hands but I wouldn't let him.

"I'm going to kill you slowly" As he whispered into my ear, he grabbed my neck, throwing my head into the ground. He went to do it again and with that tiny movement, there was just enough room for my elbow to come out, and connect with the side of his face. He flinched at the impact, and I rolled on top of him, to try and use my weight to keep him down.

He was strong, and I was so weak. I didn't want to hurt him, but I certainly had no doubt, that if I let him go, he would in fact kill me, my child, then move on to my fiends and then Dimitri. I wasn't just fighting this battle for me, I was fighting for all of them, too.

I knew I only had a little bit of energy left in me. I let my hand go to my belt where the knife was, just as Jeff gained control and threw me against the cave wall. The hit hurt more than I could've imagined, causing me to see stars. I had never, ever been in a life-threatening fight before, but I trained hard enough to know that quick recovery was essential.

I shook my head, just as Jeff came up to grab me. He lifted me off the ground by my hair, and I screamed aloud at the pain.

"I'm going to enjoy this," he told me as he went to drag me back to the cave but I kicked him so hard in the stomach he paused.

"So am I." I replied, as I brought my hand up with the knife and swiped it across his neck.

His hands immediately went to the wound, and I was dropped. I fell onto my knees, and watched him suffocate in his own blood. He came towards me again, clearly not going down without taking me with him, and I struck out again, this time slicing his Achilles tendon. He fell with one knee to the ground, snarling with rage, as his face transformed from hate to something I couldn't even put into words.

He looked like he not only hated me, but never thought this would happen to him in his entire life time. I wondered, if he died now, would he officially die if there were no bodies around for him to jump in? I wasn't going to take that chance. I rose up, legs and hands shaking, and looked at him with my own look of hatred on my face.

"I hope you die." He told me right as I jabbed the knife into his chest, aiming for the heart. I took it out, and watched his body fall, with blood cascading like a waterfall, from many parts of his body.

Feeling like he wasn't able to hurt me anymore, I sank to the floor beside the pool of blood forming. I wondered, if I just crossed the line of being the good guy and would I ever be able to return? I had never killed a human before.

Now, wasn't the time for me to dwell. Using the wall as a stabilizer, I stood and went over to grab my bag. As I thought about it, I decided, looking through the second bag, wouldn't be such a bad idea.

I found more weapons, but along with that was a bottle of water, and a granola bar. God, really did love me. Inhaling the granola bar and drinking half the water bottle took me seconds. Looking more through the bag, I saw there was a journal, and a wallet. I took both.

I walked over to Jeff's now dead body, and was a little appalled at what I had just done. I saved people, how was I the one killing them now? I shook my head, and looked through his pockets. I found car keys, and put them into my bag along with the other goodies I found.

There was only a certain amount of time before someone came to check on him, and sticking around for that would be a big mistake. Mustering up all the courage I possessed, I walked out of the cave to find my way back home.

The sun setting on the horizon, was the only indication of time passing, at a rapid pace. I was certain that if I didn't make it to civilization, I would die right here, in the forest, on the side of a mountain. It wouldn't be the worst death, but there were people counting on me. Innocent lives at stake.

Lives that needed to come into this world. Those thoughts kept me going. At times I had to pause and rest, as my ankles were still very much damaged from the melted skin. The fight left me weaker than I had ever felt, and sick to my stomach.

I stopped at a creek I found, by listening to the forests heartbeat. Water! I knew it could heal, so I limped up to it and spoke.

"Water, I know man has mistreated you, but I have always been good. Please heal me, with your powers now," I spoke softly through muffled tears, as I entered the creek fully clothed. I didn't have the energy to undress, and didn't care to. I knew I had to heal, and the water would help me as much as it could.

As I sank into the coolness of the shallow, rushing water, I felt a tingling sensation. My body, mind and soul, felt connected as the small currents whirled around my body, going in all directions.

Heal now my child, you have a journey ahead.

"But how will I find my way, water? I am lost, injured, hungry and alone… I feel defeated. Like there's nothing left."

Ask for help, and you shall receive.

I thought about this, as I made my way back to the grass, alongside the creek. I needed help, but what kind? I wasn't sure what to ask for, so I simply concentrated on getting out of the forest.

"Okay Spirit, help me out of this forest, and I will do whatever it takes, to protect the good and pure."

I waited several minutes and nothing happened…

But just then, like DeJa Vu at the cabin, a Moose appeared out of the forest, standing fierce and attentive. I had never run into a moose before, and I was stunned at its beauty.

I'm here to guide you, Emilia.

I gasped. A moose! Here to guide me? Awesome!

I tried to stand, but quickly sank, back to the damp earth below me. I was weak and the water could only do so much.

I tried again, but failed, just as I had before. I looked up, and met the Moose's eyes with embarrassment, deep within myself. How could I be so weak? How could I be so stupid!

I curled into a ball and began to sob. What am I? Who am I to think I, Emilia, can take on the entire world? Why do I think I'm special enough for that task. Maybe I'm imagining the world, maybe I'm imaging the magic.

I felt a nudge on my back and turned towards the sensation. The moose was there, nudging me with his nose.

Saying nothing, he walked away, picked a stick up with his mouth and put it down beside me. He looked at me, then the stick, and then back to me. I looked confused.

Use it.

"Use it... to.... walk?"

Yes, I gasped again, both shocked at myself for not thinking about that, and the fact that the moose was this intelligent.

I understood in a theoretical way, that all animals are tapped into the brilliant mind of Spirit, but to see it in action, was a whole other thing. I rolled over to my hands and knees which were both cut and bloody. I took a deep breath and focused all my strength on getting up. Still on the ground, I reached over to the stick, dug the end into the earth to put it upright, and used it to brace myself.

I planted one foot into the ground and forced myself to stand like a mighty oak. Finally, I was upright and even though my head was spinning, I was proud at the little progress.

"Okay... lets go" I exhaled through the words as my breathing was rocky.

The moose led me through the forest, at a pace fair enough for my condition. I was surprised at how stealthy this animal was, compared to its large size. Myself? I was loud, and clumsy.

Off about thirty feet ahead, I could see a white car through the trees. It was a chevy malibu, and a sign that civilization was close. I heard the sound of gravel, just before I saw another car pull up. I almost jumped for joy, there could be people who could help me! The moose suddenly stopped and came to stand in front of me, blocking my view of the road. My temper flared and I almost cussed the majestic creature out, until I heard the coldest voice of all.

"It will take about thirty minutes, to hike all the way up to the cave. Jeff isn't answering his phone, so something must be going on." Sylvia's ice-cold tone indicated she was not happy.

"His car is still here. He's probably just enjoying the torture." John said with a hint of amusement.

I peaked over the moose to see them, and immediately got knots all in my stomach. They were dressed in nice clothing, no damage to their skin, and most of all, energy of evil radiated off of them. They made me angry.

"We'd better get up there, I want to know what is going on. We need her to change or die, before Alexandra comes."

Sylvia began to walk and John followed close behind but not before scanning the woods. I quickly hid behind the moose, who was still standing in a protective stance.

"There's a moose over there, it's huge," John spoke, his voice carrying to me, sending chills down my spine. If they found me now, there was no chance of a recovery.

"Walk. Now." Sylvia was impatient, and I waited until I no longer heard footsteps to look up.

The moose and I both relaxed. I suddenly felt the pressure of hurrying back to my friends, and decided to get moving even though everything in me just wanted to sink into the dark realm of sleep. And Alexandra? Who was that? The name always brought pain as I remembered my missing sister, but it was a common enough name that I tried to not overthink it.

"Thank you for guiding me today dear moose, you saved my life and for that I offer you this hug." I reached out and hugged the moose. In return, I felt a surge of energy come in, that felt like everything beautiful in life. I pulled away to make eye contact, and the moose nodded as a way of accepting.

I hurried over to the car, careful enough to be quiet but fast enough, that I was there in a minute. I reached into the bag I had been carrying on my back, and tried the car keys I stole from Jeff on the malibu. They worked.

"Thank you again, God. This is a miracle."

I sighed with relief, as I opened the door. Before I could get inside of the car, a thought came to me. Once they find Jeff's body, they will quickly come down and hunt me. I pulled out the knife, I killed Jeff with and went to stab their tires.

"Shit" I murmured as I realized I wasn't strong enough to puncture anything anymore. I realized, that I didn't need to stab them, to let the air out. I went around the car and took the caps off all the tires. Surely, they would deflate in time? Whatever, I couldn't do anything else, so this would have to do.

Tired, almost dead and on a mission, I started the car of a man I just murdered, and headed back to Portland.

9. Atum

I didn't know where to go, or what would happen once I got there. I figured, that my friends would be at the rental house, worried and that would be the best place to start. But another thought came to mind. What if the Anova's, are watching them? They would notice a bloody person with a stolen car running up to the house.

I was in no position to fight, and as much as I believe Dimitri could take on the entire world, he couldn't. I also, was in desperate need of medical attention. The creek healed my wounds in the way that they wouldn't get infected and parts of the deep cuts healed, but as for everything else? Yeah, I would need a doctor.

I decided to stop at a gas station in town. I was still battered, but there was a payphone outside I could use. I searched the car for change, and to my surprise I found some. I was shocked. Jeff didn't seem like a human being, so having a normal car seemed off brand.

I looked once again in the duffle bag I took, and found the tarp. Deciding it would be better to look weird, in a tarp than attract unwanted attention, I put it around me, like one would tug a blanket closer on a chilly night. I stepped out, and went to the payphone. I dialled Dimitri's number first, and got no answer. I tried again, but received the voicemail box. This made me panic.

I paced, and tried to think of any other numbers I knew, besides his and mentally cursed myself for relying on my cell phone so much, to store all my information.

Ah ha!

Luca's number popped into my mind, and I
quickly dialled. A few rings passed and then I heard him answer in his Russian tongue.

"Allo?"

"Luca, it's Emilia. I need your help."

I quickly told him a brief recap about what happened and where I was. I mentioned my failed attempts to get a hold of Dimitri and my worry about my friends. He asked for the address to the house.

"I will have Donny go by and see what's going on. As for you, Emilia, I will come and get you. Stay put. I'll be there in ten minutes. Get into the car, lock the doors, and wait for me. Understood?" His stern manner amplified by his thick Russian accent.

"Okay, Luca, thank you." My voice sounded on the end of hysteria.

I disconnected and got back into the car. The waiting felt like it would never end, and every so often I would receive puzzled looks by the employees. I was starving and food was so close, but I only found spare change in Jeff's car, nothing substantial.

Exactly ten minutes later Luca pulled up in his black three-hundred chevy. He got out of his car, and into Jeff's passenger seat.

"I brought you some clothes, and food." He handed me a bag and spoke with a tenderness, I had never heard before. "Go change in my car, and I will deal with this stolen one."

I didn't say a word. I simply followed his instruction and got out of the malibu holding duffle bag.

I fragilely got into the three-hundred and tried my best to get the damp clothes off, without ripping the wounds deeper. I had to be extra careful around my ankles, but Luca was a smart man. He only brought me clothes that could stretch and were breathable. I dug deeper into the bag and found actual food, waiting for me, at the bottom. It was fast-food, something I didn't eat much but at this point, I would've eaten a slug.

I pulled out the burger, and inhaled it, quickly moving onto the next burger. After I polished off those, I dove right into the fries, and finished with the entire bottle of water, he put in there.

"Feeling a little better now?" Luca asked as he got into the car, I forgot to lock.

"Yes, actually. Much." I replied to him with a kind smile.

Man was I ever grateful for the people in my life.

"Donny hasn't gotten back to me on the status of the house, but he should be arriving soon. I am going to take you to a doctor I know that will help you under the table. No record or payment required. My treat." He winked at the end, and I was absolutely blown away by the animation in him that I had never seen before. I thought of Luca as a killing machine with no feelings, but maybe, just maybe... he was human.

He certainly looked like it now. Sitting this close to him, I was able to get a sense of his aura. He felt strong, but also very haunted. I looked at him and saw a man, pained with emotion, masking it with seriousness. This made me see him, not as inhuman, but as vulnerable. It made him even more handsome. Though his slicked back, black hair, light blue eyes and gold chain, did enough of that. Another detail I started to notice was the birthmark, right between his high cheekbone and right eye. It was subtle, but added something stunning... All of that, combined with a tall, lean and muscular build, was just as deadly as his fighting skills.

Of course, Dimitri was a lot bigger in size, but something about Luca made me think that didn't matter.

After my inner revelation about him, we drove to the doctors in silence. I was relieved, at not having to use my brain power. Instead, I rested my head against the cool glass of the window, and felt myself drifting away. I faded in and out of consciousness, barely aware of my surroundings.

Suddenly, I was in serious pain. I was trapped in the woods, and they were burning. Everything was burning. My skin was melting and the smell was horrifying. I heard a scream, and realized it was mine. I started to violently shake and heard another voice crying out my name. I looked around and saw no one. Then my sister appeared.

Startled, I looked around for help but it was only her and I. Alexandra stood in front of me, engulfed in the flames that weren't burning her.

"Join me Emilia," she spoke as she held out her hand to beckon me. It felt wrong and I hesitated, like maybe she wasn't here to save me. Inside of me, I heard another voice calling out to me. I listened, and suddenly held all my attention. It spoke softly, like honey dripping all over my body.

"Emilia...Sweetheart?" I felt a hand sweep through my hair and woke with a startle. Luca's face hovered closely over mine, and the sign of calm waters and life, was reflected in his eye colour. They resembled a shallow, calm sea. It seemed like the only thing that could put the trees out, were his eyes, and his eyes alone.

"Emilia, are you alright?" I looked over, blurry eyed. I saw a white lab coat, and the face of a man looking at me. I shot up, looking around to gain more awareness. A hand rested on my shoulder, "Emilia, you're safe. You're with me. My name is Doctor Shawn Mackenzie, Luca Ratnikov, brought you here." The man spoke softly, like one would with a wild animal. I looked at him, and blinked until my eyes would focus.

He was an older man, pale but not in a sick way, just in a way, that said, he would burn badly if he was in the sun too long. His grey hair was styled nicely, and his eyes shone with concern, wrapped in a soft brown colour.

The rest of his features revealed his age to be in the late fifties, but other than that, he was okay looking. The thing I noticed was a cleft in his lip, almost like someone had sliced the upper lip open with a knife.

I looked over at Luca, who stood beside my bed now, like a marine, with his hands behind his back. He wore a leather duster, and an all-black outfit underneath, paired with a big gold chain, around his neck. His hair, ever practical, styled in a slicked back manner, looked flawless, but the bags under his eyes, gave away that he hadn't slept, no matter how attentive he looked. Lastly, I looked down at myself. Bandages, covered my ankles, my knees and my hands. My eyes filled up with tears, as I remembered the recent events, that just took place.

"Oh my god! The baby! Is the baby, okay? Doctor? The baby? Oh my god…" my hands went to the tiny baby bump.

"The baby?" asked Luca, looking at me while raising an eyebrow.

"Yes, I'm pregnant. Thirteen weeks, and I haven't seen anyone yet." I told them both, looking from face to face with concern filling up my features.

"I didn't see anything abnormal, but you did take quite the beating. It would be... rare, if the baby was okay, after all the damage control I had to do. Lay down, and I will grab the equipment to look." Dr.Shawn said, as he rose to grab his monitor.

I braced myself, for what could come. If I lost this baby, I didn't know what I would do with myself. Dr.Shawn hooked up the machine, and ran a cold jelly, across my uterus. He brought down a remote looking thing and ran it though the jelly, looking for something. Through the screen I could see what was going on. This was my first ultrasound. Neat.

I held my breath as he searched for a little heartbeat. As the moments passed and nothing came to the screen, I felt more and more sick. How could I kill a man, and a part of myself too? I closed my eyes, so my tears wouldn't betray me.

"There it is, look Emilia. Open your eyes," I did as the Doctor directed and saw the little tiny baby.

I breathed. He's safe, my son, he's safe!

"Thank God," was all I could manage to say.

"Dimitri would've been very ups– oh my god! Dimitri! Sophia! Luca! Where are they? Where's Donny? How long have I been here?" I rapidly spoke the words, and went to wiggle out of the bed. The Doctor stopped me, and I looked at Luca expectantly.

"Yeah... I don't know where they are." Luca spoke to me, but wouldn't meet my gaze.

"Excuse me? You don't know where they are? What does that even mean? FIND THEM." I went from excited to very angry. "Where is your brother? Didn't he go looking for them?"

"Yes... He did. He went to the house, but found nothing but a mess. Everything was ripped apart. No one was there, but he did find a note. It's written in a language I don't know, here." He handed me the piece of paper, and I took it with my shaking hands. I opened it, with the finger space that I could. I read it over, and over. I read it backwards and forwards. Then I read it again. Without hesitating, I threw the closest thing I could find across the room – a pillow.

"What does it say?" Asked Luca, never moving from his tense posture.

I sighed, "It's written in an old language that my sister and I studied, so we could speak freely together. I don't know anyone else who speaks it... It says: To save the innocents, we need one soul, a powerful one to rule them all. Once the full moon is here, understand that death is near. Within these words, is the direction of sorrow, find the right place to end the morrow."

"It's a riddle," said the Doctor.

"Yeah, no shit, Einstein." I threw the paper to the ground, and ran my bandaged hands through my hair.

"Judging by the riddle, we have until the full moon before they kill everyone. The words say, they hold the key to finding the location, but the English translation gives no indication." I spoke with questions in my voice but everyone in the room stayed silent. So, I continued,

"Aramaic words, mean more to me. They're the language that my guides and I speak, but I don't understand, what this is telling me…" I racked my brain but couldn't make any connection.

Suddenly, a thought came to my mind. "Luca…" I asked looking over at him. He seemed ready for a world war, and boy was he about to get one. He nodded in encouragement, for me to continue.

"I have an idea, but I'm going to need your help, along with Donny's. We need to go back to that house. I have a note there, I need to find. There's someone who can help us." Myles, the old man from the DINER, in Olympia.

He spoke to me through my mind, unlike any other human, I had ever encountered, here on this earth. He warned me about the Anova's being in town, plus he already knew about them. It was time to make a call.

"Let's go," Luca said, as he walked over to help me out of the bed.

"Emilia, with all due respect, you're in pretty bad shape…I don't think you should be parading around like a superhero, when you could use lots of rest," Dr.Shawn said, as he met my eyes. They were full of concern, and I knew he genuinely, wanted to see me do better. He just didn't understand, how much was on the line for me.

I stayed perfectly still, and met his eyes unflinchingly.

"I'm no hero, Dr.Shawn, I'm out for revenge." I moved off the bed with Luca's assistance and we headed to the car without looking back.

We got back to the rental house and my stomach dropped. I felt sick and panicked as we pulled up into the arched driveway.

"Are we sure no one else is here?" I asked Luca, uneasily.

"Donny has been keeping an eye on it. He says no one has been around since he came the first time." He put the car in park and looked over at me.

"Emilia, I know you and I have only spent a little time together, before. But I know Dimitri, I've fought along side him many times, in great battles. He is a smart man. Wherever they are, we will find them all, alive."

"Thanks Luca." I said, as I got out of the car. I still wasn't sure, how I felt about him entirely, but Dimitri trusted him, and so I had to, too. Him and his brother were the only options, left for me.

As I walked up to the house, Donny opened the door.

"Hello Emilia, you look tired." He said in a charismatic way. Luca was more of a silent and intense man, but his brother? He was animated, charming and witty. Plus, they were both good-looking. But something in their eyes scared me. It wasn't a warm spark, like Dimitri had. It was more like a blank space, or a wall, that had nothing behind it.

I rolled my eyes, as I passed by and entered the foyer.

"Whoa." Was all I could manage to say. It was an absolute disaster. The once beautiful staircase was ripped apart. The marble floors, were covered in textiles and broken glass. It looked like a tornado had come through here.

"Whoever was here, must've been looking for one thing, in particular. I don't know if they got their hands on it." Donny spoke beside me as Luca entered to take in the scene.

"You two stay here, I have to run up and grab something from the room." I spoke, as I began to walk but a hand came out to grab mine.

"No, one of us will come up with you. Just in case." I turned and saw it was Luca, who stopped me.

I sighed, as a way of annoyance and agreement. He had to half hold me, as we walked up the ruined staircase. My ankles we're still weak and wouldn't hold my entire body weight.

When we reached the top, I was surprised at how tired it made me. We walked over to the room, I was using and found the way to the bed, through the mess.

"You're in bad shape, are you sure you're up for this?"

Luca asked me, as I sat down, of course with his help.

"Yes, Luca. I'm the reason those innocent people became involved, in the first place! I can't just leave them, to a fate they don't deserve."

"But...."

"No," I held up my hand to protest him, "no buts. Just action. I need some time in here alone. Guard the upstairs, and see if there is anything else that could help us."

He looked shocked, at the authority in my voice, but didn't protest. I saw a glint of amusement in his features, but he did indeed leave me alone, and he shut the door behind him.

Now in my own space, I could sit and touch Spirit. I wasn't able to feel the magic, while I was in the cave, and I had been too weak, to even think about it since my escape. But in this room, I had the space, and I intended to use it for the highest good. I sat with my legs hanging over the bed – the comfiest position, since I was pretty much wrapped in gauze – and let my mind settle into relaxation. I focused on finding the answers within, and began to breathe deeply.

In these moments, I either heard a voice, or saw an image. Neither of those things came to me, and I suddenly felt, like I lost my connection. I reminded myself, that would be impossible, and tried to sink deeper into the meditative state. Furious at my inability to receive a message, I got up and wobbled around, trying to pace, but it was failing.

"Why? Why? Why? What the hell is going on?" I mumbled into my hand, as I chewed on my nails to calm my nerves.

I decided to try again, but this time I needed to be more relaxed. I moved all of the ripped pieces of my clothing, off of the bed and laid in it. I took deep breaths and focused on a solution. I went deep into meditation, even past the point, I thought was my deepest yet. Suddenly, I got an image in my mind.

It was a being of light, one I felt like I could trust. I looked around, and saw we were surrounded by four pillars of marble and gold.

"Whoa, what is this place?" I asked aloud to myself. To my surprise, the being replied.

"We're in the four pillars of health and vitality, Amona."

"Who's Amona? I'm Emilia." I looked around, confused.

The light being suddenly turned into a man. The first thing I noticed were his eyes. They shone great wisdom, highlighted with amber iris', that didn't even look real. His skin was vibrant, and from his tone and face structure he looked Egyptian. But considering, he was just a ball of light, three seconds ago, I didn't know where he could be from.

"Ah, you have not gotten to that part in your journey yet.

We will meet now, but you will understand later. I am Atum." He grabbed my hand, and started humming the most beautiful sound I had ever heard. Simultaneously my body began to vibrate. It felt like my cells started to dance, reacting to the sounds and his touch. I felt like a happy plant, when the sun was shining.

"What are you doing?" I asked, puzzled.

"I am healing you." Atum smiled, and showed off his dazzling perfectly straight teeth.

"Why?"

"Because you asked for it, Amona." He dropped my hand and I felt the last wave of vibrations fade. I was still humming from the healing, feeling more alive than ever.

"Who are you?" I gasped, trying to figure out how, I even ended up in this gorgeous place.

I decided to move and walked up to touch a pillar. The smooth marble, felt amazing on my skin, and the gold looked more beautiful, than I had ever seen before. I looked up, and saw a ceiling made of the same thing, paired with engravings. Each looked like the map of the stars, but was even more complicated. It all looked like a web, that was interconnected to everything else. Truly, this was the most stunning place I had ever been before, in my life. I looked down at the floor, to see if the engravings were there, too. Sadly, it was all plain marble, but to my surprise, there were scattered red rose petals, laid on top of it. This gave it, an alluring contrast.

I looked over at Atum, who looked at me with ease and delight. I felt this need in my body to hug him. I needed to be close to him.

"You can hug me," he said, as he opened his arms up.

"How did you know...?" Shock ran though me. And as I wrapped in the embrace, I lost that anxiousness.

"We are all one, Amona. Come with me, I want to show you something." He turned to walk and I followed.

We came to the corner, where another pillar was standing graciously, and sat on a bench made of gold.

Atum went into the pocket of his white robe, that was tied with very simple braided yarn, and pulled out a piece of crystal, Amethyst I believe.

"Amethyst's, are great for keeping one sober, in the body and in the mind. You will need this for your next task. You can activate its powers, by asking it for help. Make sure, at all times, it is touching your skin." He handed me the stone, and I flipped it over, in my hands. I realized then, that my hands were healed, and the gauze was gone.

"Why would I need it? And you still haven't answered my question about who you are."

"I am everything, and I am nothing. You must figure out what that means for yourself."

"Okay, sure. I also have another problem. Can you help me figure out, what I need to do next, to save my friends? I don't know where they are, and I don't know how to find them." I asked pleadingly. If we could be sitting on a bench of gold, I'm certain this guy, could help me in some way.

"Trust your gut. Follow your intuition. It will lead you there. It's time for you to go back now, Amona. Remember, you need to take care of yourself, as well. I am always here, ask and you shall receive." He got up, kissed my forehead and faded into a light being again.

I got up too, puzzled, as to how I was supposed to get out of here. I thought about returning to my friends, and miraculously the pillars began to fade and I was back in the bedroom.

"What is going on..." I whispered aloud to myself. I was getting used to my powers, and the situations that came with them, but what just happened here? Yeah, that was beyond me.

"Luca!" I yelled, and waited for him to find me.

He opened the door in a flash, ready for a fight. He was beside me, in no time, and as I looked up at him, my heart ached for Dimitri.

"Are you okay?" He asked as he assessed my limp body. I didn't bother to move, I just laid there, like a starfish.

"Yes, I'm fine. I need your help. I want to shower, but I'm full of gauze."

"And... you want me to?"

"I want you to help me, take it off, obviously." I rolled my eyes at the question.

"Emilia, I don't know if we should." He knelt down, so we could be at an equal level.

"I need to clean myself Luca," I started to cry heavy tears and I could see the outburst of emotion, made him uneasy. He stared at me, a few more minutes, and then began to take the gauze off my hands first. When he was done, he moved to my ankles, and I heard him gasp.

"What? What's wrong?" I asked, shooting my head up.

"The skin, it looks almost... healed." He sounded puzzled and I didn't believe it. I sat upright and looked for myself.

"Oh my..." I touched the light pink skin. No wounds were to be found. I looked up at Luca, confused, then back down to my ankles. I ran my hands over them again. I looked at my hands next, and saw no cuts or bruises.

"Atum..." I breathed out, my eyes full of wonder. Could that meditation, have brought me somewhere where I could've been healed, in the physical?

"Who's Atum?" I heard Luca's voice, but didn't react. I was too, in awe. I looked around the room for verification, and saw the Amethyst, attached to a necklace, on the window sill, next to some broken glass.

Whoa.

10. Deep Wound

   I hated to waste time, but I had to admit, that showering was the best idea, I could've ever come up with. After everything I had been through in the last couple of days, I was surprised, I even knew my own name anymore.

   So many things had happened that made me question everything, I previously thought I fully knew and understood. Of course, you can't know everything. There are things I don't even know, that I don't even know but that wasn't the point anymore. The point was, that time seemed inconsistent with my mind, and everyday seemed like a month, had passed between them.

   I sat on the edge of the bed, in the destroyed room, wrapped in a towel with Atum's Amethyst, around my neck.

   The cold air coming in from the broken window, kept me alert, and felt like a cold cloth on my mind. I decided to get up, stepping around the mess, to get to the openness, that was the window frame. I couldn't open the window because it was smashed, but I didn't really need to. It was broken enough, that a human could fit through.

   It was time to get to work. I searched the room for clothes that were clean, and good to wear. Most of the clothing, I brought with me, were ideal for this kind of situation, but they were ripped or covered with dirt. Finally, in a drawer that looked like it had been gone through, I found a decent pair of jeans and a t-shirt, plus one of Dimitri's hoodies I stole. I got dressed, and then searched for Myles' number. It wasn't left on the note he gave me, so I had to try something else. I went over to the room, Elizabeth had been using, and searched for her cell phone. Unfortunately, when I found it, the screen was smashed into pieces. Great.

"Is there anything they haven't ruined?" I asked aloud, looking up to the ceiling, like it would start to spell the answer back to me.

"Not really," I almost jumped out of my skin, at the voice from behind me.

"Donny! What the hell. You scared me."

"I know, you weren't paying attention at all. Hasn't Dimka taught you anything?" He laughed, and took a step closer to me.

I crossed my arms, "Yes, he has. Excuse me, for letting my guard down, for four seconds."

"Hey, Emilia, I'm just playing with you. I know you're smart, and very resourceful. I came up here, to ask what you wanted to eat. Luca and I are hungry, and we figured you would be as well." He touched my arm to try to calm me, but all I felt was a slimy feeling.

"Yeah, I'm starving. Pizza?" Easy, and they usually delivered. My diet was a mess, but that seemed to be accurate, for the way my life was going.

"Pizza it is, Queen E. Are you going to come downstairs? We cleaned up most of the mess there, so we could all be comfortable." He asked as he bowed and headed to the door.

"I'll be down in a minute, shut the door." I asked him as he walked out.

He did. Then I was back alone with my thoughts. The most dangerous thing to be in a room with, at times. I would've rather tried to fight a bear, than my inner turmoil tonight, but I just wasn't that lucky.

"Ah ha!" I rejoiced. A bear. Animals! Why, are they always my last thought when I need help? I thought hard, about what animals could travel between Portland and Olympia.

I heard a tiny knock on the window, and opened my eyes. A sparrow was there, looking at me through the glass. This window hadn't been smashed, amazingly. I walked over and opened it up.

"Jack?" I asked the cute little bird and I extended my finger for him to hop up on.

Yes. You called?

"Yes. Jack, I need your help again. I need you to get a message to a particular human in a town, a little ways away. Can you do that for me?"

I can do my best. Show me the message.

I thought hard about what I wanted Jack to do. I needed him to get a message to Myles, the brilliant man who held answers. I showed Jack the image of the man, and then, let him know, I needed Myles to somehow help me.

Jack gave me a slight nod and then flew away, harder and faster than I had ever seen a bird go before. I exhaled and relaxed, slightly. I was doing what I felt was right.

We were three days before the full moon, which meant we were that much closer to my friends impending death. That much closer, to possibly losing the love of my life, and the father of my child. I walked down the hall, to the beautiful staircase, that I had once been in awe of. It held the same elegance, as the first time I laid my eyes on it, except this time, I felt only pain. How had things gotten so terrible, so fast? I suppose I wasn't sure how this would end anyways. I had been hunted, for so long, that confronting the people doing it, seemed like such an enormous task, never mind the added pressure of innocent lives being at stake.

I walked downstairs, grateful for the smell of fresh pizza, that wrapped around me, like a comforting blanket. I saw Donny and Luca in the kitchen, strategizing, and again felt a surge of pain in my heart, from the absence of Dimitri.

"Here Emilia, we got a bunch of different kinds, we weren't sure what you would like." Luca said to me, without meeting my eyes. He slid over a plate, and I didn't hesitate to fill it up with pizza. I went to sit in the living room, and practically inhaled my food.

After I finished, I sat back, and watched the fire they made, in the pit dance. The oranges, reds and yellows intrigued me. I was so concentrated, that I didn't even noticed Luca sit across from me, until he spoke.

"Are you sure you're up for this? I don't know what we're walking into, and if you get hurt...." As he broke off, he averted his eyes, away from mine. It was very uncharacteristic of him.

"Are you scared of what Dimitri will do to you, if I do?" I teased.

"No. I'm scared of you getting hurt." He said in a serious tone.

With that, he silenced any witty comeback, I could think of, leaving me to stare at him in disbelief.

"What? Do you think I want you, to get hurt, Emilia?" He asked, shock hung in the air from his tone, but his face was perfectly still as he spoke.

"No, I just don't see you as a person capable of emotion." I retorted, without any thought, of how the words might have made him feel. For a moment, I saw a glint of hurt in his stone-cold eyes, and remembered the moment I realized, how vulnerable he was in the car.

Before, he was only a man of war. A man who would go out, and do what needed to be done, no questions asked. He was a great ally, to have on your side, and the worst kind of enemy, any man would dream of. I only saw him capable of getting a job done, and being efficient at doing it. Now I looked at him, with conflicted feelings.

"I don't feel because when one emotion is let in, they all come in. Then, I have to see myself, for what I've done. I don't want to do that." He met my eyes in a heavy gaze, that sent butterflies in my stomach.

"Luca, I'm sor-" He held up a hand, to silence me and I obeyed. Deep within me, I was still frightened of the brothers.

"You will sleep down here tonight. Donny and I will switch, between watch." He got up, and went to a pile of blankets, and a pillow. "Here," he handed them to me.

I grabbed them and nodded in agreement. I then realized, I was still in jeans. I rose from the couch, only to be stopped by Luca himself, holding a set of pyjamas. I looked at him puzzled, and he placed them into my arms.

"Goodnight." He said, and turned towards the kitchen.

"Wait, Luca?" He turned back around.

"Yes, Emilia?"

"The duffle bag I had in the car, when you picked me up, is it still in there?" I remembered the stone, that looked like the galaxy, was inside of it. I didn't know what it did, but maybe it could be helpful, in this mission.

"Yes, why?" He arched an eyebrow in curiosity.

"I need it. It has something I think may be of use to us."

Without even realizing it, I grabbed his hand and looked at him pleadingly.

He looked at my hand on his, with a conflicted look on his face.

"Can you get it for me?" I asked with a sweet voice.

"Tomorrow. You need to rest." He knelt down in front of me and kissed my cheek. Another thing, that surprised me.

"Okay, fine. Goodnight, Luca. Night, Donny." I called over my shoulder.

"Night Queen E!" I heard from a distance. I smiled. Luca took this as sign, and got up to leave towards the kitchen. I watched him walk away and wondered what it was like to be him.

I changed into my PJ's and tucked myself into my make shift couch bed. With the fire pit, I felt oddly calm, like death wasn't riding on the back of my heels. I slipped into sleep easily.

"Emilia," I woke to a touch on my arm. Luca was standing over me, with a concerned look on his face.

"Yeah?" I asked, looking around to take in my surroundings.

"There's a man here named Myles. He says you called him and asked for help." I blinked a few times, to gain some clarity. Luca was standing over me, with his arms crossed, in clear disappointment. He was intimidating.

"Yes, I know him, and we need his help. Let him in and I'll be right back." I threw the blankets off and rushed up the stairs to get dressed. I walked into the bathroom, of the room I had stayed in, and was again amazed at how beautiful it truly was. Luckily, my hair brush was still there, though I think someone had cleaned it. I thought that was weird.

After I finished battling the knots, caught in my long dark hair I went to change. I found myself staring at the little details, that showed how my body was changing over the course of time. I was amazed, at how resilient this baby was. I honestly didn't think he would have made it past the cave situation, but here I was, growing and changing because he wanted to come into this world.

"Truly remarkable," I whispered. I couldn't let this baby, grow up in this world, without a father. And I for sure, couldn't let all of my innocent friends, die. I took a deep breath and headed back downstairs to make a plan.

I ran down the stairs, and found Myles patiently sitting on a bench made of oak in the foyer. The strong contrast, of the stained cherry wood against the marble was brilliant.

I had to admit, it made Myles look extra wise.

"Hello, Morgan Freeman," I extended a hand for him to shake, but he promptly ignored it and went straight in for a hug.

"Hello, young lady. What kind of trouble, have you gotten yourself into, now?" He pulled back and smiled. I couldn't help but chuckle. Myles could read my thoughts, so I knew he would already be caught up, on most of the things I had been thinking about, while he was in the house. The baby, saving everyone, the Anova's, ready to kill everyone, for a reason I still didn't understand.

"Let's take a walk in the backyard, and I'll explain everything." I said to Myles, as I started to turn towards the yard.

"We'll come with," Luca spoke from beside me. He was more tense than I had seen him.

"No, Luca, I'll be okay. You and Donny stay in here and just watch." He eyed me very suspiciously, like he didn't believe I would be safe, ten feet away.

"Luca ease up, she can take the old man." Donny said from the front door. He was relaxed and leaning against a marble pillar.

Myles stood there patiently, and didn't bat an eye, at the bickering. I imagined he was reading everyone in the room's thoughts. I looked back at Luca, and for a moment I saw a flash of guilt, behind the once dead eyes, I feared. He simply nodded his head, in agreement. I took that as a sign and led Myles, to the garden.

"Is he always so intense like that?" Myles asked, once we were safely out of ear shot.

"Oddly enough, no… He's been extra uptight and I can't figure out why." I turned thoughtful, but Myles' laugh, snapped me back to the moment.

"Oh, Emilia, you are so wise, yet so young, at the same time! Let's get down to business, and you tell me, why I'm here – besides the urgent matter of the Anova's, kidnapping your friends."

"I knew you would be reading everyone's mind," I rolled my eyes, and he simply shrugged. I pointed to a bench beside the garden. We sat, and I began to tell him everything, that had happened. He was patient, with my flare-ups of emotion, and nodded along, as I told him all of the things that had happened, from the moment the four of us women left Olympia, to the present moment. I filled him in on what happened at the cave last, because I wasn't sure, I was ready for him to see me in that light.

"Which brings me, to how I got out of the cave… It was very weird, Myles. I didn't have access to anything, so I used the tools I had. I was almost out… But suddenly Jeff appeared, out of no where." I started to shake, and he put his hand over mine to calm me. I smiled and pushed myself further. "I had to fight him. I was so weak, I was sure, I was going to die. Then, suddenly this dark feeling welled up inside of me and I knew.." I sighed, "I knew I had to kill him, Myles. And so, I did." I started to cry real tears of agony, at this point. Everything I had been feeling inside of me, just burst out, in that moment of admission.

Myles put his arm over me and held me, until I calmed down. The worst part, wasn't even saying the story, out loud, it was not saying the things I felt about it. I felt guilty, yes. But, a tiny part of me liked it. I liked killing Jeff. It made me feel powerful, like I could do anything. And that? That was the worst part, of the whole thing. Of course, Myles probably knew, because he could read minds, but I hoped somehow, he couldn't read mine.

"You did what you had to do, Emilia. It's okay." I looked up, and he had an honest look on his face, that wasn't full of anything, except understanding, like he knew exactly what I was going through.

"I wish I could read your mind, Myles." I chuckled.

"You can't? I haven't been able to read your thoughts, since I arrived, so I assumed you learned how to control that power." His puzzled expression, mirrored mine. I shook my head.

"No, I don't know how to do that. Yet." The slight optimism, brought me back to the reason we were both out here, and I didn't even think about why he couldn't read mine. "The reason I asked you to come, is because of our conversation at the diner. I remember you told me about the owner being kidnapped, and then the Anova's, showing up. I think somehow those two things might be connected."

"Why do you think that?" He asked, surprised.

"Honestly, I don't know. Just this weird gut feeling.

There's also a riddle they left us. Here," I handed him the tiny piece of paper, the old Aramaic language was written in.

He took it, read it over a few times, and handed it back to me.

"How many people do you know, understand that language?" He asked, his seriousness raising concern.

"Two. Myself, and my sister. Wait no, three, including you, and four with whoever wrote that." I was confused.

"You know three people, Emilia. Out of the three people you mentioned, you've met, who could've written that note?"

"What? I don't have time to play games, Myles. I don't know who could've written it. I'm assuming you didn't write it, I didn't write it, and Alexandra is dead." The anger in my blood began to boil and I stood up, to start pacing around the blooming spring garden.

"Is she? You mentioned the dream you had about her, the one where she was asking you to come and join her. You mentioned that Sylvia spoke her name, when you were escaping the mountain. And the most important fact here is: you don't have any proof, that she died. No one ever, found her body." His words sent chills down my spine, and I had to come to a stop to look at him.

"Are you saying, you think that MY sister wrote that?" I shouted, so loud, I heard birds fly away. The raising of my voice, made Myles flinch, but that didn't stop him, from standing up to meet my gaze.

"I'm only stating what you already know." He grabbed my hand, and suddenly images started flashing through my mind.

There was one of Alexandra, that day she went missing. We were in the woods, and she was talking to the birds. Then again, at moments, when I had feelings of her watching me. The next image, was of her in the dream, trying to get me to join her… And the last image, was of her writing this note inside the house, with Sylvia beside her and Dimitri, thrashing around in handcuffs in the back.

"…What the hell" I spoke to no one, and my voice carried the lost and empty emotions, I started to feel.

"Emilia, today, there isn't enough time to go through, how I know this. There is only enough time, for you to think about where your sister would be, and what she wants."

Myles took my hands in his, to try to get through to me, but my mind was reeling.

How could he think, Alexandra was behind this? Here, this man I've spoken to twice, is asking me to think completely different, of someone I grew up with. Someone, I'm related to! How could this be? He was lying. For all I knew, he wrote it, and was trying to throw me off his tracks.

"Get off of me!" I shouted, as I took my hands violently out of his. I saw the hurt in his eyes, but he obeyed me, and stood still.

In a flash, Luca was outside, standing in front of me, in a protective manner.

"Don't be so dramatic, Luca. She's fine, she's just in shock." Myles spoke confidently, but I could see a glint of genuine fear, in his eyes.

"What did you do to her?" He asked, keeping his body positioned mostly in front of mine, with little room for me to see the conversation, take place. Not like it mattered, my head was somewhere else completely.

"I told her a truth she didn't want to hear, because she needed to hear it. You could learn something, no?" After that, Myles' voice, became nothing to me and I wandered away.

Faintly, I heard my name, but I didn't know who could be yelling it, at this time. I walked towards the front of the house, unsure where I could go, that would make sense in this world. I was pregnant, alone, and hunted. I didn't truly know, any of these people. What had my life come to?

I walked out of the gate in a total daze, and came to an abrupt stop, at the end of the driveway. I tried to feel anything but all I could feel was nothing. This was truly a breaking point in my life.

11. Facing Fear

I walked helplessly for whoever knows how long, and eventually came to the cool forest floor, in a fetal position.

It was ironic, because as I grew a life inside of me, mine was anything but growing. I laid there, and cried, until the tears became a pool of hopelessness, masked with my faint sobs, that rang through the forest like the flaps of butterfly wings.

I heard a stick crack, and it jolted my eyes, to where a wolf came, stepping slowly, so as not to scare me but with a look that chilled my blood. The wolf's eyes were a glowing amber, like sap, that looked right through me, ones I had never seen before. I didn't dare move.

The wolf came to stop, five feet away from me, and looked down from her higher position.

Amona, please.

The strong female voice rang out to me.

I looked at the wolf, puzzled at the use of the name that was spoken to me, only ever by Atum, a few days ago.

"That's not my name," I whispered.

Amona. It is time for you to get up.

"No."

Amona.

"I don't owe you anything!" I shouted with pain and fear making my voice tremble.

You don't owe anybody anything. But, you owe it to yourself.

This instantly made me mad and I shot up.

"Owe it to myself!?" I screamed, and started to pace,

"Myself? The one who has gotten herself in trouble many times over! The one who got her friends, and the love of her life kidnapped? The one who is crazy enough, to think she can talk to animals, and feel the earth? Yeah, I owe it to her all right! I owe her a night, at the insane asylum. What am I even doing here? WHY, AM I HERE? Huh? Can you answer that, because I doubt my existence everyday. All that has happened, has only caused me pain, my whole life, and now I am told, my sister is the one doing all this to me? I owe it, to no one, because I am no one. Just a stupid pawn, in this elaborate game, called life. They win. I quit."

I came to kneel with my arms spread wide, in a merciful position, in front of the wolf. Those dangerous eyes locked mine. She let out a deep growl, from her throat, and I was finally ready for things to end. I waited for her to rip me apart.

Then an explosive white light blinded me. I blinked until I could see again, and in front of me stood Atum, the same man from my meditation.

I gasped.

"Amona. Enough is enough, here." He extended his hand, and I stood up. His presence was so overwhelming, I couldn't help but listen.

"How can you be here?" I asked. Baffled that one moment there was a wolf, and the next, a man, in white robes.

"I am that I am. I can be everything all at once. Now is not the time to explain, Amona. You have to believe in yourself. There is a reason you are here, and you have to find that reason, within yourself. Sometimes, we have to be shaped by challenges, that feel like they are ripping us apart. Those are the ones that will put us back together, in a different, stronger way." As he spoke, he wiped away a tear, that escaped my eye.

"Why do you keep calling me Amona?" My voice shrunk, as I asked the question. I was no longer feeling as bold and angry, as I was a moment ago.

"It is an old name, from a far away land. It means, 'the hidden one.' It was your first name, long ago." He explained with a kindness in his voice that soothed me. He cupped his hand around my cheek, and held it there.

"My first name?" I looked up to meet his blazing amber eyes.

"Yes. When you first came to earth. Amona is a very special name. At that time, you were forbidden to use your talents, from fear of others, who would take it from you. I believe you refer to them as the 'Anova's.' They've been hunting you and others like you for thousands of years."

"What?" I couldn't help but express my absolute disbelief. I grabbed his hand from my face, and held it.

"I will always speak the truth." He looked deep into my eyes, and the image of a woman came. She was in the desert, crying the same way, I just was. She cried out to God with her hands full of sand, and I watched as her faith, like the tiny pieces, slipped through her fingers to become nothing.

Atum continued, "You have never been as strong, as you are now. That is why, all of this has been made extra hard, because they have lost their grip on you. You have tasted freedom, you have tasted pure connection, and you crave more. It is in you, to connect with consciousness. You are deep rooted in this Amona, and you will do great things, to change the course of humanity forever. All you need to do, is step into your power." I shivered and dropped his hands.

"What if I can't do it? What if the thing I face, are too much for me to handle...." I started to sob again, and Atum wrapped his arms around me, in a warm embrace. My head rested on his chest. I breathed in a scent of frankincense that hung around him.

"There is nothing you can't handle, when you come with the power of love." We stayed like that, for a moment, and then another flash of white happened, and suddenly, I was back outside of the house, in the city without Atum.

I looked around and saw nothing, but the fading sunset, and the faint moon above. It reminded me, that we only had a day left, to save the people I love.

"Come, with the power of love," I said aloud, just as I heard the far away howl of a wolf. I smiled and took a very deep breath.

If I believed that I wasn't good enough, then surely, it would be true. But, if I loved myself enough, to know that I could do anything I set my mind to, then surely, that too would be true.

I headed toward the front door.

"Emilia!" Myles came running out, wearing the face of someone who was deeply stressed.

"Hey Freeman, I'm so-omph" He ran right into me, to give me a giant hug. I said nothing and held him back in an embrace.

"Don't apologize. I shouldn't have been so inconsiderate, in my words. I'm sorry!" He pulled back and held me by my shoulders, in a serious way, a grandfather would talk to his granddaughter.

"I forgive you. Thank you for telling me the truth, when I needed to hear it. I would have been blinded this whole time, but you helped me see through it." It was true. If I would've seen Alexandra as a surprise, I'm afraid I would have not been able to react properly.

He held me and smiled bigger than I had ever seen before.

"Myles, there's something I need to show you. I could use your help with it." He dropped his hands from my shoulders, and stood attentively. I motioned for us to go inside.

Walking in the doorway, was more and more surreal each time. Donny stood diligently at the top of the staircase looking down at us.

"Emilia. Welcome back." He nodded, with only a trace of his charisma shaping his lips into a smile.

"Where's Luca?" I looked around to see.

"In the living room." Donny nodded his head to the direction.

Myles and I began to walk, and he whispered in my ear.

"There is something weird about that kid." As he shook his head. I said nothing, but silently agreed. I had always felt a little off put by Donny. When we got to the living room, Luca was sitting on the couch I slept on, with a blanket I used, draped over his legs.

He was staring down at it with so much concentration I was almost afraid to speak.

"Luca..?" His head shot up and his eyes went wide.

"Emilia!" He threw the blanket off, rushing to stand in front of me. Completely ignoring Myles beside me. He grabbed my wrists tightly and brought them up to his chest.

There was so much anger in his eyes, that I was truly afraid of him, in that moment.

"You're hurting me." I spoke to him in a calm voice. It seemed to register and he loosened his grip.

"Emilia. You can't run off like that, in times like these. What if something happened to you! None of us knew where you were. Do you understand how scary that is? How worried I was?" He spoke rapidly. His Russian accent made the words, mold all together, in one long sentence. I didn't know how to respond, so I just stood there, baffled at all the emotions, on his face.

"I'm sorry, Luca." I was on the verge of crying, but didn't want to show my anxiety.

He kept his gaze locked with mine, and at one point the tension became too much, I had to look away. I looked at where my hands were held at his chest, and noticed where he put them. He held them right where his heart was.

I looked up, with total shock and he let go of my hands and walked back to the couch.

"What do you need?" He called back to us.

"We need that duffle bag, please." I looked at Myles who was watching Luca, very tentatively. He eyes followed every motion.

Luca picked it up and put it, on the coffee table.

Myles and I, sat opposite of him on another couch.

The lights in the house were bright enough, but I needed some natural lighting.

"Can you get the fire place going?" I looked up to Luca, who's eyes were on me.

He said nothing, stood up and began to assemble the indoor fire.

I searched through the duffle bag, trying to keep my mind from returning to that awful night. Memories would come rushing back, so I had to keep reminding myself that I was no longer there, and I was safe with these men. My hand finally touched what I had been searching for.

"Here, is what I need your help with." I pulled the egg-shaped sphere out, that looked like the galaxy was held inside of it.

Myles gabbed it, and tossed it around in his hands a few times. He lifted it to the light, then back down to the floor, in the shadows. He put it to his ear, then brought it to his nose to smell. He shook it and shook it until he finally came to a conclusion.

"It contains magic," he said, still holding onto it, to study it.

"Yeah, I figured. I used one of those, to burn the metal I was chained up with. It didn't look like the sky, though it looked more like melting lava, or like the sun was trapped inside." I gave a little more detail, to how I used it that night in the cave.

Myles turned inwards, to think. I looked over at the fire Luca had built and felt a pain in my heart, from all that had been lost.

"Emilia, come here my love." Dimitri said to me one day, as we camped outside in the luscious green mountains of the Pacific North West.

I went to sit by him on a log, he put in front of the fire, he just built. He wrapped his arms around me and I rested my head on his shoulders. We sat there in silence, all night, watching the stars dance in front of our eyes. The galaxy was visible, and it felt like I melted, right into it. When it finally vanished and the moon came up, I felt an entirely new cycle of life, come into our lives. It was one of the most magical nights, of my existence.

I came back, the present still holding a piece of that night with me. Then, an idea popped into my mind.

"What if it somehow contains properties, of the night? What if it makes, whoever is using it, invisible by blending them into the dark?" I turned towards them both, in an excited manner. I was remembering all the power I felt, as I connected with the lava stone, and how fiercely it worked, to do exactly what I needed.

"You think so?" Myles still held the stone, and was turning it over as he spoke his question.

"How would that even be possible?" Luca looked extremely skeptical.

"Remember what I told you about the cave? I had to really connect with the stone, and then throw it at the fire, to burst the magic out of it. When I did, the magic worked, along with the fire, to do the unthinkable. It melted my chains, but didn't burn anything else. What if this stone works, the same way? What if we can use it, to cover us, so that we look like the night." I was almost out of breath. This would give us a huge advantage, if we needed to sneak up, on the Anova's.

"Only one way to find out." Myles tossed it to me.

"Bring it with us, when we go. But for now, let's make a plan to get our friends back. Donny! Get in here." Donny came into the room, after Luca's call, and we began to plan.

Today was the day, we all faced our enemies. Some of us, were more used to it than others, but it didn't mean, the tension wasn't high. I took one last look at my changing body in the bathroom mirror, before heading out. The subtle changes never ceased to amaze me.

Today, I wore black jeans, a black turtle neck and a zip up coat that was, well, black. We figured if we all dressed in black, it would be less easy, to see us, in the full moon night.

If my theory about the stone was right, our outfits wouldn't matter, but Luca didn't want to leave anything to chance.

"Ready to go champ?" Donny nudged me as we walked to the car.

"As ready as I'll ever be, Donny." I forced a smile back at him. Myles and Luca were already waiting beside a new blacked out Suburban, the brothers were able to get over night. I didn't even bother to ask how.

"Luca?" I asked, nervously.

He paused from putting things in the trunk and looked back at me.

"Thank you for helping me. You were the only person, I felt I could call, after I escaped that cave. You have been so supportive through all of this, and I just wanted to tell you, I appreciate you." I went in to give him a hug and he stiffened. I dropped my arms in shock, but respected his resistance.

"Emilia... Dimitri is a good friend of mine. I would do anything to help him. But you? I would die for you. Don't forget that." He shut the trunk and got inside.

I stared after him, with my mouth wide open. Where did that come from?

Forcing myself into action, I took one last look around, and got into the car. It was time for real life to happen.

"It's three o'clock now, which means sunset will be, in five hours. The note wasn't clear on timing, but I am assuming they will drag this out until midnight, when the moon is at it's highest." I slipped into leader role, from the backseat of the car - much to my dismay, I wanted to at least be up front.

"The location you told us about, is roughly a four-hour drive. Are you sure, that's where they'll be? It seems, quite a distance to go." Donny asked from beside me, in the back, opposite of Luca, driving in the front. The brothers, figured this would be the safest, they could keep me. Myles sat in the passenger seat beside Luca. He seemed comfortable, but I could tell he wasn't.

"Yes. It's one of the reasons I asked Myles to come. The owner of the diner, disappeared around the same time I went 'missing.' He owns lots of land near Olympia. Myles has been there before. He has a house and lots of land surrounding it. Right after the Anova's, ~~the~~ found my camp, they went directly there, which makes me think those two are connected." When I first met Myles in the diner I thought, that was just a freaky coincidence. Since then, I've learned that there are no such things.

"She's right. The timing is a coincidence. Throughout all of my lives, I have come to learn that nothing is a coincidence." Myles voiced my thoughts and looked back to smile at me. All my lives? Did Myles have access, to his past life memories? I pushed that aside, as a 'later' question, I would get to.

We drove in silence, all tense and ready for action. The closer we got to the destination, the sicker I felt. Everybody, except me, would be apart of the extracting team. My job, was the use my powers, as a 'lookout.' How lame.

Since Myles could read minds, he was a great asset, to go in. Their plan was to free Dimitri first, so he could fight, assuming he was in any condition to do such a thing. I had a feeling he wasn't, but I knew he would try. He was a true warrior.

Trying to soothe my nerves, I decided to look out the window, and watch the trees go by. Much to my surprise, I saw a wolf, running along side the car. It looked over at me and I saw those same majestic amber eyes. Whoever Atum was, I was seriously impressed. What did he say to me? 'I am everything and nothing. I can be everything all at once...' I wonder what that made him. I touched my hand to the Amethyst on my neck, and watched the wolf fade into the forest. I had a feeling that wouldn't be last time I saw her.

Myles? I tried to reach out to him. I waited a few moments, and when I didn't get a reply, I tried again.

Myles? Can you hear me?

Nothing.

I touched his hand, and he looked back at me. Maybe I needed eye contact.

Myles?

He studied my facial features for a moment. It was like he thought he knew, what I needed, but couldn't quite get it.

He looked me over and over, then titled his head to the side, when he saw the Amethyst, around my neck.

"Where did you get that?" The sudden sound aloud, cut through the tension in the car, like a diamond cutting glass.

"Long story." I said, how could I even begin to explain that, never mind in front of the two brothers.

"Make it short." Myles looked at me again, the same way he did, when we first met at the cafe. I could tell he was trying to read my mind, but this time wasn't succeeding.

"I got it from a man named Atum." No need to mention where I met him.

Myles stared at me with wide eyes and an open mouth.

He didn't move any part of his body. I finally decided to say something, once he looked like he had stopped breathing.

"Myles? What's the matter?" I asked, uneasily. I wasn't really sure I wanted to know the answer.

"Atum?" He asked, coming back to normal.

"Yes. Do you know him?"

"Do you know what Atum means, Emilia?"

"No? It sounds close to Atom though, but he doesn't look like a chemistry equation, Myles. Can you cut to the chase please?" I asked, rolling my eyes.

"Atum means God in Ancient Egypt." He said with his voice full of wonder.

I gasped. Holy! Literally.

Everything was starting to click… In the image, he showed me of Amona, she, or I, was dressed in clothes, I only recognized from Hieroglyphs. She was crying in the dessert, to God. Atum healed the worst wounds I had ever seen, and every time he spoke, I felt calm and at ease. He effortlessly went from a female wolf, to a male human, in seconds. Plus, he brought an object from my mind to me. Not to mention, he knew things I didn't even know, I had to know.

"Whoa," I breathed.

Myles caught my eyes, with the most excitement I had ever seen in a human. His usually wise, dark brown eyes, now shone with a youthful brightness I was happy to see.

"We're almost there." Luca's powerful voice, brought us all back to the mission. His thick Russian accent was hard to ignore, especially when his voice was serious.

About ten minutes later, we came to a stop on a road, Myles let us know, was close enough to the house on foot, but far enough back, that we could escape quickly.

"Us three are going to go in. Emilia, it is so important that you stay here. I want you to use that stone, to try and blend the car, to be invisible. I don't know, if I believe in this, but if anyone here can figure it out, it's you. Let us know if you see anything." Luca handed me an ear piece, and I put it on along with everyone else. I wasn't super happy to be left behind, but I knew being the lookout was an important task too.

"What else, can I do to help?" I asked Luca, yarning to be apart of the action.

"Stay safe." He looked at me and smiled. Something completely out of character for him.

Donny got out of the car, and Luca followed. Myles sat behind, a few extra seconds.

"Emilia, if Atum gave you that necklace, it's important that you keep it on, at all times. Whatever purpose it will serve, is a big one. Use the stone like Luca said. If something bad happens, call on the animal spirits. They will help you."

I nodded in agreement, and then he leaned back, to give me an awkward hug.

I stepped out of the car, to get into the front, but Luca stopped me. Before I could ask why, he pulled me into a tight hug and I heard him smell my hair, in a deep inhale. I looked up to see his face, and I could've sworn, there was a peaceful look on him. He was full of surprises tonight.

"Thanks Lu–"

He leaned down and kissed me. Not just a soft kiss, but one with the same amount of force, as a semi truck hitting a small car. He kissed me with so much feeling, I thought I was going to fall over right there. Before I could even stop it, I felt myself react to it. I was suddenly kissing him back, with the same amount of force and I didn't want it to stop.

He broke away, and let his hands drop, from where they were laced into the back of my hair. He smiled and then walked to the front of the car, to summon the others. They all waved back to me and then headed towards the house, far away in the night, leaving me in total shock.

12. The Anova's

Waiting in the car was pure agony. Every second that went by, felt like an eternity. I was reminded again of how time never seemed to be a linear concept, but rather a loop, that did whatever it wanted with you, whenever it felt like it.

Emotions attached to time, were even worse. Now almost everyone I loved, was in one place all together, fighting for their lives. I tried to tell myself, they would be fine, but honestly, I didn't know if they could be, after all of this.

I took the egg-shaped stone, out of my pocket and was suddenly reminded of Elayo, one of my ancestors. Last time I spoke with him, was when I first found out, Sylvia was in charge of this mission to hunt me. I remembered the words he spoke to me, *illubi a shami fur elitar*. Thinking of them now, made me realize what they meant. Illuminate me for protection. Elayo somehow knew the language, this stone would understand... I spoke the words and concentrated on what I wanted it, the stone, to become.

Then, in case that didn't work, I said, "Cover me, like a blanket in the night, wherever this stone is, the night follows." I repeated this ten times, and each time I felt more and more, of an energy surge. On the tenth time, I spoke, I felt goosebumps rush throughout my body, and hoped to God it worked. I myself couldn't tell, but I had a good feeling.

A few more minutes passed, and I started to grow uneasy, but then voices started to clear on the ear piece.

Most of the things being said were at a calm level from strangers, so I assumed my friends' presence, wasn't known yet. That was the whole plan, really. Find Victoria, Elizabeth, Sophia, Janica and Dimitri, then free them without anyone seeing.

Suddenly I heard a commotion of some sort, but no fighting sounds. I took it as a sign they found them and were freeing them. Since Myles was with them, and could speak through the mind, he was to send telepathic messages to everyone. The plan never included speaking aloud. I heard footsteps and a window opening. Then I heard nothing at all.

The ear piece went out abruptly and I froze. It suddenly felt like I was back in the cave with Jeff, and had no connection to anything. I got chills all over my body, and a sick feeling began to come up. I slumped in the seat to hide from anyone looking. I was so scared, I didn't even feel like I could call upon the animals to help, for fear that the thoughts alone, would alert the Anova's.

I waited about a minute, before I dared to look again, then I saw a moving shape. One that was loud and clumsy.

The shape kept falling, as it ran towards where I was. Then I realized who it was.

"Sophia!" I hopped out of the SUV and ran toward her.

She kept running past me, like she didn't even see me.

"Sophia!" I yelled. She stopped and looked around with tears streaming down her face. She was a total mess. On her face were signs of fatigue, malnourishment and dehydration.

"Emilia?" Her shaky voice tried to find where my voice was coming from.

"I'm right beside you, Sophia, can't you see me?" I was confused. I could see her perfectly, in the moonlight. The blue contrasted her light brown hair, in a way that made it look almost pale blonde, and her pale skin looked almost translucent.

"I can't see you." She put her hands over her eyes and I saw burn marks on her wrists. I grabbed her hand and pulled it away from her face. She looked and finally saw me.

I quickly grabbed her and pulled her into a hug. I steered her towards the SUV, and couldn't help but notice how in the moonlight she looked beautifully haunted by fate.

"Emilia…. We…. Have….. To… Run!" She said to me as she cried in my arms. I picked her up and placed her in the backseat. I got in with her, fast enough, that only God could've seen, what just happened.

I immediately took off my coat and put it over her. I sat beside her and assessed the damage further. It looked serious, like they really wanted to hurt her, but knew they had to keep her alive. My blood started to boil.

I handed her a water bottle and some food we packed, but didn't hesitate to jump right into questioning.

"Sophia, where is everyone else? What happened?" I asked sternly.

"I think they're all still inside trying to get out. I got out of the window, then I heard this big crash. Myles told me, you would be here and to not look back, so I didn't. I just ran and ran and ran…" She started to sob deeply, while looking at nothing ahead of her. They were, the signs of shock, coming over her, but I needed to know more.

"Sophia, I need you to focus." I touched her leg and she flinched, but relaxed slightly, "how many Anova's were there?" That was the only thing that mattered. How many enemies was I about to go face.

"I don't know.." She shook, and I squeezed her leg, lending her my strength, "seven, maybe eight."

Those were not good odds, for my friends.

"Listen to me Sophia. I'm going to go in there, and get the rest of our friends. I need you to take these car keys and if anyone you don't know, comes to this vehicle, or I'm not back in fifteen minutes I want you to leave. Do you understand?" I handed her the car keys, and cupped her face in my hands.

Her only acknowledgement of my words, was a slight nod. I kissed her cheek, and ran out of the SUV.

I didn't have time to be scared, I only had time to be courageous, and believe all of the words Atum said to me.

I started towards the house at a full sprint pace, and remembered the image of the wolf in my mind, from our ride here.

Wolf, I need your help.

I heard another stick crack and looked to my right. Glowing eyes shone going at the same pace I was, and for a moment I didn't know where I ended and the wolf began. We became one.

I need you to call your pack. I need some of you to guard the SUV. This is the time, to rip anybody apart, who tries to hurt that innocent girl, got it?

I understand. I heard back, and then I was no longer running with the wolf.

I got to the front of the house, and assessed my options.

I knew the layout, from what Myles had explained to us, but if my sister was behind this, I knew it wouldn't be easy. I knew there would be a trap, and I would have to be prepared for it.

The intensity of this night, reminded me of a game my sister and I used to play in the woods, where we grew up in Alberta. She and I would be on opposite teams, hiding from one another in the forest, until one of us was caught or it got dark.

"Emilia…" she would taunt me, "I know you're out there, come on out and we can end this game."

I would never give up easily, but she would beat me, more often than not. I always had a soft spot, when she would pretend to be hurt. I would always fall for it.

Not tonight.

I spotted a room with the lights on, and saw some of my friends trapped in there. I could see Sylvia Smith, all covered up, with her old body looking like a vulture, ready to pick apart its prey. To her left I could see John, the other soulless man that wanted to torture me. A couple people, I didn't recognize stood upon them, but no sign of my sister.

My eyes fell onto my friends, Myles, Victoria, Janica, Donny, Luca, and Dimitri…

He was as dashing as ever. I don't think, there would ever be a moment in time, where he wasn't the most beautiful human on earth. He was visibly tired, and his shoulder length hair was a total mess. He was covered in bruises, and the white tank top he had on was dirty, and stained with spots of blood. My heart ached for him.

Wait. We were missing someone. Elizabeth!

Where is Elizabeth?

I didn't know to whom I was calling, but someone ought to hear me.

To your right, keep going. She's crouched behind that big tree.

I quietly walked over and whispered, "Elizabeth?"

A fist came flying at me, but luckily, I expected her to be there, so I dodged it.

"It's me. Emilia." I told her, as I had to dodge another attack.

"Show yourself," she said. I stood directly in front of her.

"I'm right in front of you Elizabeth!" My whisper turned into a quiet shout.

"I can't see you." She reached her hands out and I grabbed them.

"Ah!" Her shock ran out into the night and I pulled us behind the tree further, to keep our cover.

"Shhh, I don't want them to see us."

"You came out of nowhere! One minute I didn't see anything, and the next you're holding my hand."

I finally realized it. The stone! It must've worked. Where this stone is, the night follows. Each time they touched me, they were able to see me. I didn't know, if that meant we both became visible, or invisible, but I was glad at least, I was undetectable if I wasn't touched.

"It's okay, I'm here now"

"Oh my God, Emilia..." She gave me a big hug, and then looked at me with her eyes wide open. "We have to run."

Her voice became full of panic.

It's funny because yesterday in the meadow I swore to Atum that I wanted to run. I wanted to be anywhere but here, facing my problems. But, this being the second time, my fears were vocalized back to me, I realized I didn't need to run. I needed to stay and fight.

"No. You need to run to the SUV Myles told you about. Sophia is in there, and you look like you're in better shape. Elizabeth, there is a gun in the glove compartment in the SUV. Use it if needed. Go there, NOW." I put as much force into that last word, as I could. She nodded and snuck off, in the right direction.

Elizabeth is joining Sophia, wolves. I hope they heard me.

Knowing this stone held this much power, I started to believe more and more, in myself. I was tired of feeling like a pawn in someone else's game. I was tired of being afraid. I wasn't a pawn. I am that I am, which is a strong unlimited being, only subject to what I hold in my mind. And my mind right now? It screamed to let my own power out.

I let out a last prayer, to any of the spirits listening.

I know I have been afraid for a long time. I'm afraid right now even. I know that this is the right thing to do. I know that these innocent lives, need to be saved. I will do what is necessary. Protect me.

We are with you, Amona.

I opened my eyes and chills ran down my spine. I was one with my power.

I stood beside the tree and waited. I waited to hear anything, that would give me an idea, on where to go next.

"Go look for them!" I heard Sylvia's voice ring out, just as a door slammed and a woman I had never seen, walked out.

She was shorter than I, but had a build like a football player. Her curly red hair hung just above her shoulders, and she looked around forty.

I decided, if I was going to win this game in the woods, I would stop being a player and start being a maker. I picked up a piece of wood and snapped it in half with my hands. I moved to the opposite side of the tree, where I could spring and properly attack her. I watched, as I got her attention and she stalked towards where I was.

She was careful. She watched everything around her, and barely made a sound, herself. On her waist I saw a gun, but I could only assume, she would have another weapon on her. It was unlikely, anyone would come to a fight, with no weapons. Even I had one, that no one knew about.

As soon as she was within reach, I snaked out and punched her right in the face, then grabbed her by her throat and lifted her up to my eye level against the tree.

Pure shock ran through her features. Then as she figured out who I was, she started to smile, blood dripping into her mouth. We were under the tree, out of the moonlight, but the light coming through the leaves, was enough for me to make her face out.

"How do I get the others, out of here?" I asked. It was the only question that mattered, but I knew she wouldn't be much help. I was stalling.

"You're going to die, Emilia." She smiled even wider.

"Unlikely." I retorted. I went to grab her gun, but she head butted me and I lost my grip on her. It was never easy, getting hit in the face. I recovered quickly, and we circled each other. I guess once contact was made, the illusion of the magic wore off. Good to know.

"Why can't you see that you are outnumbered? You're hopeless here. Everyone you love, is going to die tonight. You can live, Emilia. You can live, like one of us. You will never have to die in your body. You can take bodies. You can do amazing things. Your strength increases, your speed, your sense of sound, sight. Everything is better when you are immortal in the body." She reached out for a kick but I dodged and shot one back, landing on her outer thigh.

I stayed calm. I wasn't a pawn in a game. This was my life and I wasn't going to let anyone take it from me! I felt this rage well up, inside of me. This uncontrollable anger, came out and I leaped at her. I tackled her to the ground, and punched her again, and again. She overpowered me, and threw me off of her. I landed on my back and looked over to see her, coming towards me. The blood in her mouth was amplified by the whiteness of her smiling teeth.

She looked like a true psycho. She knelt down to pick me up by my neck – the irony – and threw me against the tree.

"I.." I muttered.

She looked puzzled, "What?"

"I…I.." I muttered again trying to lean closer, to talk to her.

She leaned right into me and that's when I knew I had the proper chance. I visibly didn't have any weapons because the brothers didn't want me to fight, but what they didn't know, was I could make weapons out of anything.

Before leaving, I took apart a razor and held the blade carefully in the mouth.

As soon as she was close enough, I moved the blade from my gums, to between my teeth and slit right across her throat.

She dropped me, as her hands went to the wound I just made. As soon as I was free, I put my hands over her mouth to keep her quiet. Anova's, never looked like they felt anything. But when I killed Jeff, there was the same look of absolute fear and shock, that this woman held. I guess we're all afraid of something.

After she stopped moving, I kept going. The adrenaline in me, wasn't ready to quit. She wore a long trench coat, that was exactly what I needed. I searched her and found a knife, along with the gun, I had already spotted.

It was time to make a scene. I cut up the coat with the knife and used it as rope. I hung her upside down from the tree and moved a few feet away. I shot the gun off, in no particular direction. The door opened and John ran outside towards the hanging woman.

To my amazement he didn't see me, as he looked around, at possible places I could be. He looked at her, with a blank expression, and murmured something aloud. After he finished, I watched lights go from on to off, in the house.

I had to make sure, I didn't come into physical contact with him, so I quietly turned and headed off in a direction, my gut feeling kept telling me. According to the description, Myles gave us, the mansion had multiple bedrooms. One of which was extremely secure, from the inside. My first guess, was once you saw someone hanging dead upside down on a tree, that would be the first place to go.

I watched as John continued to look around, then Sylvia and another person came out. That made four, including the red head. This meant, two more were inside. Right on queue, the light in the fortress room, came on, dragging my attention upwards, toward the bedroom.

I could see a way to get up there, but it meant I needed both hands to climb. I was happy to be invisible but I still knew there were risks, and I wasn't quite sure, the full extent of the stones powers. If I made a noise, or fell, I would be at a huge disadvantage... I needed something more.

Ah ha!

Rabbit. I need a rabbit!

I waited and watched, as John scouted the area. He was thorough in his search, and his proximity was making me anxious.

I heard leaves and whipped my head around. Three rabbits sat at the forests edge.

I smiled.

All I need you to do, is run in the direction of the east. Run along the forest perimeter. Can you do that for me? Please.

We can! Three voices replied to me. Then they took off.

I heard their feet rumble the leaves and catch John's attention. His eyes fell, just above where I was, and went along with the running of the rabbit.

"She's in the trees! Let's go!" He yelled and took off towards the sound, with a tall man beside him. Sylvia didn't move. She just stood, staring at the lifeless body hanging from the tree. I had a feeling, Sylvia didn't believe for one second, I would ever leave Dimitri behind.

I had to act fast. I quickly hoisted myself up the brick wall, which thankfully had a lot of ledges. The room was only on the third floor, and took me less than a minute, to get to the window. I peaked inside and almost fell right back to the ground.

Sitting on a bed in the corner was my sister, Alexandra. Right beside her was Dimitri.

She sat and smiled at him, touching his hair, and whispering in his ear. I thought I was the most disgusted at that, but the look on his face, showed he was even more disgusted.

Besides Alexandra, there were two other Anova's, with her. One was a very tall woman, probably six-foot-two-inches, who looked like she benched twice as much, as my body weight. Her hair was tied back in a tight ponytail, which showed just how thin it was. She wore a suit that matched the man beside her. The first time I saw Jeff and John they were wearing matching suits, but these ones were made differently. I was starting to wonder, if they were split into some kind of teams, or cult levels.

I looked a little more, and saw everyone's hands, were tied behind their backs. Great, another thing to overcome.

I breathed a heavy exhale, and my breath stuck on the glass. I knew people who were trained were made to see every detail, and I was counting on it.

Beside me on the ledge, was a corner I could back into, that extended to a roof of gravel. I knew, that my chances of fighting up here, were not very good, but hey, that was the theme of the night.

I heard the window crack open, and watched the shadow of a head, look right, then as it was turning left, I gripped onto the above ledge, and led with a kick to get inside. My foot connected with whoever's face, as I flew into the bedroom. I didn't have time to process it, I took the knife out and stabbed the heart of the body, I just tackled. I stood up, and saw the shock on everyone's face.

I caught the sight of the suited man on the floor, and leapt at the woman next. She was fast, and she saw me coming. Apparently, my stone illusion had worn off, the moment I crashed in.

She drew her gun instantaneously, but I didn't plan on dying from a gun shot. I went for it, but smarter this time.

Once, Dimitri had shown me what to do, when someone pulled a gun, and I brought that memory back up. Using all the force in me, I was able to get it out of her hands.

From behind me, I heard this evil laugh, come from Janica. It was high pitched yet dark. I couldn't spare a glance. I had an opponent in front of me, that was the immediate threat. Everything else, I would get to later.

Don't kill her. Atum's voice rang through my mind and I paused.

Why?

Once the body an Anova, is in, dies, they can jump to another one, that is in the room. That is why I made you wear the Amethyst. It protects that, from happening to you.

I was distracted with this new revelation, that the woman got the drop on me. She punched me so hard in my face, I thought my neck was going to snap. Blood started to pour out of my nose, faster than running water. I dropped the knife and lost sight of it. The taller woman reached out and picked me up, by my hair.

"Ouch!" I yelled. How unfair was that?

Slow claps came from the corner where Alexandra stood.

"Well done sister. You had everyone here scared, for a moment. Then, as always, you failed." She gave me a fake, pouty face. It was the first time since I was a child, that I had seen her. She looked the same but, different. Her blue eyes, no longer shone with life, they were bleak with death. Her black hair was long and beautiful, but didn't seem like the silk it used to. She wore an elegant black dress. It reminded me of a dress, a witch would wear.

"Huh." I chuckled. The slight movement hurt, from where I was being held, by my hair.

"Huh, what?" She asked, mockingly as she rolled her eyes.

"Everyone kept calling me a witch, yet here you are." I looked at her in astonishment. The pain was totally worth the comment.

She marched towards me.

"Drop her." Alexandra spoke to the woman. Then literally, she dropped me to my knees, then walked to stand behind me.

"Leave her alone!" Dimitri shouted.

Alexandra didn't take her eyes off of me, as I got up.

"So, what's your plan Emilia? John and the others, are right outside that door, waiting to come in. Your friends are all beat up. One of them, has even lost her soul, when you stormed in and murdered Michael." She pointed at Janica, and I glanced over to where she sat on the bed, with the others. It terrified me. She sat there pleasant, with a cunning grin on her face. Her dead eyes shot back to me.

"I don't have a plan." I spoke with sadness at my carelessness that resulted in the loss of a friend.

I turned back, to face my sister. I took in as much of the surroundings as I could, without looking like it. The window was still behind me, with the woman standing between me and it. The other's, sat on the far-right side, with a very large bed and a small window. Beside them, was an Anova, living in Janica's body. And to the left, was the door, with more people waiting, to come inside. I needed time.

"What's your plan Alexandra? Kill everyone and have me convert to your little cult? What's in it for you." I crossed my arms over my chest.

"Exactly the plan." She nodded.

"But why bother? What am I to you?" I asked.

"You are really nothing to me. But to the Anova's, it means extinguishing the blood line, that runs deep in this world. Every time one of you," she spat at the word "comes back to earth, you bring goodness with you. Goodness with that much power, offsets everything we're trying to accomplish. You are very powerful, as you are, but when you join us? You will be ten times more powerful. You will be a god, Emilia. Plus, I get to level up, if I convert, such a high profile like yourself," She smiled and began to pace "Remember our last day together?"

"Yes." I replied

"Well, that was the day, life changed for me. I was taken by John and Jeff. They thought I was you. They brought me all the way to Portland, to meet Sylvia. Immediately, she could tell, I wasn't who she wanted but she knew I was just as powerful. She told me her plans, for you. I simply said, if I joined I could be worthy to her cause. I wanted to be just as powerful and immortal as she, so I made her a deal. If I find you, then convert you, I get to fast track my levels. From then on, we worked together, to bring you, to this very moment." She came to a stop, right in front of me, and I felt sicker, than ever.

"You disgust me." I spit blood onto the floor, in protest of her words.

"Oh, well. Sandra."

The woman behind me, put me into a headlock. I struggled against her, then relaxed as I remembered I would need my strength. Alexandra walked over to Janica, and cut her ropes.

With free hands, Janica was instructed to take the knife, and hold it to Dimitri's throat.

"No!" I started to thrash.

"The note was clear. We need a powerful soul. If you don't want to come willingly, then we will have to force someone else, by process of elimination." Alexandra spoke those words coldly.

As soon as the blade touched Dimitri's neck, he moved in a maneuver, I thought would get him killed. Instead, all of the men were in sync and started to work together, to get free. I forgot that Myles could read minds!

I saw them move, so I made my move too. I wrapped my foot around Sandra's knee, and pulled as hard as I could.

When I felt her budge, I threw my elbow back, and connected it with her temple. I wiggled out, and punched her as hard in the face, as I could manage. I kept punching, until she went limp. I didn't forget the message from Atum. I spun to see Alexandra, almost at the door, so I grabbed Sandra's gun and shot the roof.

"Don't even think about it you psycho!" I yelled at her.

"What are you doing to do, Emilia? You would never hurt a fly, never mind kill your own sister. You're too soft." She taunted me.

I heard pounding at the door, and knew time was ticking. From the side, I saw an unconscious Janica or Michael. Whatever, it was now. I was just relived they didn't kill it.

"You're wrong." I shot her.

But not in a fatal place. I shot her in the knee cap. She screamed in agony but was still mobile. She tried to get to the door, so I shot the other knee.

She fell to the floor, in a fetal position and began to cry aloud, in pain.

"You stupid bitch! You will never make it out of here! I will make sure your entire bloodline does, and you along with it! You will never, ever come back again."

Luca jumped up and dragged her away from the door.

He put her beside the bed, and then grabbed a dresser, to fortify the doors strength.

I ran over to Dimitri and jumped into his arms, into home at last. He hugged me back, like this was the only important moment all night. I pulled back and looked into his eyes without conveying any words. We didn't need to.

And we didn't even need psychic abilities. We just knew each other that well.

"I hate to bust up the reunion but how do we get out of here?" Luca came in and snapped us both back to reality.

"Good question, Luca." I mumbled aloud.

13. The Amethyst

The five us sat there and tried desperately, to think of how we were going to get out. Luckily, the pain and blood loss Alexandra was experiencing, made her pass out, so we had one less thing to distract us.

"What about the window?" Donny spoke to us.

"No, if someone is out there, we're dead." I said to them all, my mind reeling from everything going on at once. "Plus, I think now, that they know I'm here, the stone won't work."

"Wait, it worked?" Luca looked at me with both eyebrows raised.

"Yeah, long story but I was only caught, when I came into contact with someone." He nodded to acknowledge me, but I could tell his mind was in shock.

"What if one of us distracts them, by trying to negotiate at the door?" Myles looked at me and I shrugged. This was out of my league.

I looked over to the bed and saw Victoria sitting there. It reminded me, that she was in the room. I walked over to her and knelt to look her in the eyes.

"Victoria," I spoke softly, grabbing her hands between mine. She was staring at the far wall, looking away from all of us. Behind me, I could hear the Anova's, still trying to get through the door. Whoever had this place built, really made it solid.

"They're going to come in, any minute, Emilia. They're coming for us. They will never stop." She spoke in a scary tone, I had never heard before. It was like a ghost from the future, was speaking a fate, no man would wish for himself.

In the midst of the chaos, I stopped for a moment and thought about this. They would come for us again and again. Even if we planned an accurate escape, who's to say they wouldn't find us, in a car? Or maybe they already got to our SUV, and we had no hope, out of here. How long had it been since I told Sophia to leave if I didn't come back?

Were we already out of time? I did the only risky thing, I could think of.

"Okay, if they're coming, let's get ready for them." I said to Victoria as I rose. Her eyes became sharp again and fixed, on my rising body.

I turned to face the men, and held up a hand, to stop their argument. Dimitri in an uncanny way, faced me at that exact moment. His gorgeous forest eyes shone, as he stared. The rest of them followed suit and quieted down.

"What if we don't run? What if we simply get ready to fight our way through this house? We know they have us cornered. We know they have more man power, and weapons than we do, but you know what they don't have? Power to an unlimited source of love. We can overcome anything, when we fight out of this. Love for each other, and love for humanity! There is no use running. Believe me, I tried, and look at where I am now," I gestured around, "the same place they wanted me, in the first place. So, now my friends, I ask, are you ready to fight?"

Victoria stood up and grabbed my hand. I looked over at her and she simply nodded with a determined look in her eyes.

"I'm always with you, Emilia." Dimitri came to stand, in front of me. What he did next amazed me. He bowed in front of me, then put his hand over my stomach. He then smiled, a soft smile, that I rarely saw on him in a public space.

"We're in." Luca said, in a matter-of-fact voice, from across the room. Donny simply nodded.

"What can I do?" Myles asked as he observed everyone in the room.

I had to think quickly. They all looked at me for this plan, which I didn't even have yet. As I started to think, I realized there were many ways out.

"When I was kidnapped, I murdered Jeff by myself and his spirit wasn't able to take my body... I don't know why. I have this crystal from Atum, which makes it impossible for the Anova's, to enter whomever is wearing it. So, if I'm protected then I can give this crystal to someone else. And, I can try to use my power, as a shield, for whoever is with me. Let's split into teams."

"I can use my powers to protect myself and another. I don't think I'll be able to use them, for more than that. I'm already exhausted." Myles piped up.

"Perfect. Myles you team up with Victoria. Donny, you take this crystal, and stay with Dimitri, in here, to take out whoever comes through that door. Luca, you come with me, and we will distract the others outside somehow." I told them uneasily, barking orders made me seem confident, but I had no idea, if this was going to work.

"No, Emilia. Dimitri should be with you. You need to stay safe and keep the family together. Donny and I can handle whatever." Luca spoke softly to me and met my eyes. They held emotions, I was just getting used to seeing on him. The vulnerability made him handsome in a way that I never thought possible. It was truly shocking, how complex this man in front of me, truly was. I felt bad, I had never given him much credit.

"Okay, Luca." I nodded, and felt a slight twist in my stomach.

From there, everyone went to their posts. Before I headed to the window, with Dimitri, I walked over to my sister, to say goodbye. Who knew how tonight was going to play out. I wanted to get some closure and mourn her fake death. Plus, I didn't want anything to come and haunt me down the road.

I looked down at the life bleeding from her and couldn't help but notice a necklace around her neck. It was one my father gave to us, as a family honour.

"Emilia!" Dimitri's voice, snapped me back to the mission. I grabbed the necklace off Alexandra, and stuffed it into my pocket. I decided to check all her pockets, and found a folded up piece of paper. I took it to read for later. Dimitri had grabbed the weapons, from the other bodies. It was our job to start shooting out the window, while moving along the side of the building. Then, we had to somehow manage to get off the roof, and to the SUV.

While we were doing that, Luca and Donny were going to move the dresser and unlocked the door to the room.

They then, were going to hide. Once the Anova's got in, their job was to ambush, and kill whoever they could.

Only one of them was protected, with the crystal and it made me uneasy to think about. However, once Victoria was safely out of the room, Myles was going to protect

Donny, from a distance. Again, no clue if this plan was going to work, but it was the only one we had. I had to trust they could handle it.

"On my count..." Dimitri whispered to me. I crouched by the window sill, with my back towards it. Dimitri was right beside me, waiting to cover me, as I slipped into the night. I was so terrified, I thought I wouldn't be able to move.

"Three." The word jolted something inside of me. Suddenly I was on the move, with gun shots, firing from behind me. I heard them but didn't look back, as per instructions. I climbed out the way I came in, and slithered down the side, behind a bush.

A voice was shouting, "They're on the move! They're outside!" And I knew, step one, of the plan, had worked. A thud beside me, let me know Dimitri had finally joined me, earth side, and we moved like a cohesive unit in the night.

Gun shots were flying, but they didn't even come near us. I had a feeling this wasn't a coincidence. He and I, ran as fast and as hard as we could. We didn't look back, and so far, we didn't see any other Anova's.

"Umph!" The cold hard ground connected with my face, as I tripped and stumbled to the ground. Dimitri stopped and leaned down, to pick me up. Thankfully he did. In the moonlight, I saw a movement of light come from the trees, and a gun shot went off.

"There's more!" Dimitri yelled and pulled me into his arms. I heard more gun shots go off, and I looked up at Dimitri. He sat with me, in his arms, back to the forest. I could see all the love in the world, in his eyes, as he looked down at me, then blood started to come out of his mouth.

I heard a curdling scream and realized it was my own.

"Dimitri! NO!"

"Emilia... It's okay. You need to run... Go my love..." He tried to push me, but he didn't have much strength left. The bullets sat in his back, creating wounds in my heart.

"Never." I knew I didn't have much time. I heard footsteps coming towards me. I did the dumbest thing ever.

I stood up. Immediately, two flash lights shone at me, and I looked down at a dying Dimitri. He had fallen into a fetal position and the look in his fading eyes, told me he was terrified to watch me die, much like I was to watch him. I looked back up and said nothing, as they closed in on me.

They came closer and closer, and as they did, I grew more and more still. I was so calm, that time seemed like it didn't even exist. All I knew, was that no one I loved, was going to die, right now. I summoned up, all of my will power. I called upon every being I could think of. I called Elayo to be with me. I called Atum, to heal Dimitri. And the best part, I called the wolves. Glowing eyes popped up in the forest, but I was too focused on my targets. I heard growls from behind me and knew a part of the pack was there, waiting for my signal.

Beyond the Anova's, I saw Sylvia Smith, standing on the forest line, with a smug look on her face, that I couldn't wait to wipe off. This whole time, she cried about her nephew being with a witch, but didn't hesitate to have him shot.

A taller, more built man, came to grab me, but I reacted quickly.

I was banking on the fact Dimitri's body wouldn't last longer than theirs, because killing them was the only option I saw. Without further instruction, I moved to get closer to Sylvia, taking the first man out swiftly and without much effort. The other man came to get me, but again I was too fast and too focused. Before both of us knew it, his head was between my hands, and a loud snap was the only sign, I needed to know, that he was dead. He was down faster than I ever thought possible.

I looked up to see a horrified looked on Sylvia's face and moved quickly to get her. She turned and started to run towards the SUV. There was no way I was letting her out of my sight.

Emilia, you cannot leave Dimitri's body there alone! Atum spoke loudly to me.

I needed Sylvia to feel the pain I was feeling. To know what it was like to be hunted! I was so close to her, fleeing body that I could tase victory.

Emilia! Enough! A hard wall hit me, in the thin air and I stopped running. The realization came, of what was going to happen, if I didn't get back there in time.

Finish her far from the SUV, and bring me back something to show. I thought out to the wolves.

After that, I saw them all run towards her. I would have vengeance either way. Tonight, I would run back to Dimitri, the one person in the world I never wanted to see like this. I knelt down, beside his bleeding body, and put up protection just in case.

"Dima..." I touched his face, and moved his long hair away from his eyes.

He looked up at me and smiled. I could tell he was just happy, I was okay, and that these fleeting moments of his life, weren't his main focus.

I heard footsteps running towards me, and was relieved to see Luca, Myles, and Victoria.

"Where's Donny?" I asked, surprised to see the others without him.

"Oh my god, Dimka!" Luca yelled, "help me get him to the car, now!" His strong voice made us all move. In unison, we were able to lift Dimitri's, six-foot-five-inch body.

"The SUV is so far Luca, we're never going to be able to make it." I grumbled, as I tried to not think of my dying fiancé. "Stop talking then and work faster!" He yelled at me.

We kept moving, but every once in a while, we heard a groan from Dimitri. Thankfully that meant he was still alive. When we finally made it to the SUV, Sophia and Elizabeth looked like they were going to pass out from the stress. We had to put Dimitri's body in the back seat which was no easy task. Once he was fully in, I kneeled beside him.

Everyone else, piled into the trunk, except Luca, who was driving. I heard a jumble of voices speaking, but none of them were important.

"Where are we going?"

"Where is Janica?"

"What happened to Donny?"

"Is Dimitri, going to be okay?"

Dimitri and I, held each others gaze, and I tried desperately to grasp anything in the world that made sense. I could feel my eyes filling up with tears, that seemed to keep pouring down my cheeks, no matter what I told them to do.

"Emilia?" Myles peered over at me from the backseat.

"Yeah?" I managed to say, without breaking my gaze with Dimitri.

"Can you heal him?" He asked softly.

I frowned. "With what?"

"With your power." I looked up to briefly meet his eyes.

He flashed an image in my mind, from the night I went to see Atum, at the four pillars of health and vitality. I looked at him confused.

Call the healing energy to you, energy knows no bounds. Myles spoke to me in my mind.

"Who has the Amethyst?" I asked.

"Donny." Luca's voice broke as he spoke the brother's name, we just left behind.

Can I do it without the crystal? Myles met my question, with a confused look of his own.

You have nothing to lose if you try, and you have everything to lose, if you don't.

I grabbed onto Dimitri's hand and took a deep breath. His eyes began to flutter, and I could tell he was losing consciousness. There wasn't much time left for him. I began to steady my breathing. Inhale, exhale, inhale, exhale. I went deep into my body. I could feel the pulsations of blood, rushing through my veins, like a raging river. My intention was set on healing Dimitri, and only that. I focused my whole being so intensely, that I forgot I was inside of a body. I didn't feel like I was anywhere, instead, I felt like I was everywhere.

I began to feel a warm sense of knowing. Shortly after, I felt myself walk into the place I had first met Atum, the four pillars of health and vitality.

"Atum!" I called, walking around to find him.

"Yes?"

I spun around and saw him, flawlessly leaning, against one of the marble pillars. For the first time, I was taken back, by how good-looking he was. Maybe in the past, he didn't come out as sharply as a human, but now he did. His skin was the most perfect shade of caramel. His hair was long, silky with a bit of curl to it. There was no sign of age, decay, or disease on him, only pure youth, shining from his pores, that were also perfect. His eyes were so deep, yet so light of an amber, that it didn't make any sense. It looked like I was looking at fossilized maple with streaks of sun rays. He wore his usual white robe, but today the material looked like silk. He was gorgeous.

"I.. uh..." I needed his help, right?

"Yes, I saw what happened. Why are you here?" He asked me.

If he was all-knowing, how come he didn't already do, what he knows, I need him to do?

"I cannot do anything unless it's asked, Amona. Ask and you shall receive. Free-will, is the greatest gift of man kind."

He spoke softly to me, in his melodic voice, that made every word drip, liquid gold.

"Can you please heal Dimitri?" I pleaded.

"Only he can ask for help." He strode towards me.

"He's dying! How can he ask for anything!" My temper flared up, and I was ready to kick down these stupid marble pillars.

"Why don't you bring him here and he can ask for himself." Atum grabbed my hand and suddenly Dimitri showed up. He looked just as good as Atum, in my eyes. His shoulder length brown hair hung in perfect loose curls. His deep forest eyes were soft and offset by the jade highlights. He stood taller than Atum, and was more physically built with muscles. This Dimitri wore a black hoodie and a nice pair of jeans, which resembled nothing like his body in the physical world right now. I decided to look down at myself, and noticed I wore a beautiful silk red dress, that showed all my curves off, including the tiny baby bump.

"Where am I?" Dimitri spoke, while looking around.

"You are in the four pillars of health and vitality, Orion."

Atum looked at me and just shook his head. Clearly, he knew what I was going to ask.

"Who's Orion? Emilia, why are you here?" He came closer to me, but didn't touch me.

"Dimitri, you're here because you need help. You're dying on earth. I cannot heal you, without your permission. Dima..." I grabbed his hand and cupped my face with it.

Dimitri still looked confused.

"Come, let me show you something. Amona, stay here." He led Dimitri away and I watched as they walked the same tour, I first went on. The anxiety of this whole thing, was killing me, so I began to pace. The cold marble floor beneath me, made me realize I didn't have shoes on. Why didn't I?

Being here, made me think again, about time. It seemed so irrelevant. How is it linear, if I could be in two places at once? I was almost certain, time was a constant loop, playing over and over again. Maybe this is the loop, I was destined to live. Fight or flight. It seemed so miserable.

"Emilia, come up here." Atum signalled me, to meet them by the back pillar – my favourite one. It stood as tall as the others, but what made this one special was the gold zig-zag line, that went through it. It resembled a lightening bolt through the marble, and it was the only one that was unique. All the others were smooth with no imperfections.

I joined them at the golden bench. As I was about to sit, Atum got up.

"You know what to do, Emilia. Follow your heart." He kissed my forehead and became a ball of light that floated away.

I turned to look at Dimitri who was looking down at his hands.

"Can I heal you?" I asked politely.

"Emilia, I have failed you." He spoke with deep pain in his voice.

"What are you talking about Dimitri?" Shock ran through my body. He just took several bullets for me, that was the exact opposite of failing me.

"I should have known about Sylvia. I let them get the best of me, and now everyone has suffered for it. You are suffering, I can see it in you. Donny has paid the ultimate price. And those friends you made? None of them will ever be the same, again. Hell, one of them was taken over by an Anova! You should let me die. At least, I will die an honourable man and father," he looked up at me, with tears in his eyes. They showed so much pain and sadness.

"Dima... you did your best, with what you had. You can't beat yourself up about it." Delicately I placed my hand over his.

"It wasn't good enough. Let me die this way, please Emilia. At least, I would have died for the most important people in my life." He turned his face away and began to stare into space. I felt pain in my heart, over his emotions. I could feel them eating him up inside, and truly I wanted that pain to go away. Perhaps letting him die, was the best thing to do for him... No. I wouldn't leave here until he healed. His life was just beginning.

"Dimitri. Enough is enough. You will not die here today. You will be reborn. You said it yourself, 'a father.' Do you think I am going to let you give up, on being one, before it even happens! You are insane. Look at me, when I'm talking to you!" This snapped him, out of this trance. His eyes fell upon me. I could only imagine, what he saw.

My long light brown hair, in a style I couldn't quite see, but knew it was perfect. My deep blue eyes with crystal highlights, full of passion and love for him. My skin, so perfectly tanned in the four pillars, showcased beautifully against the silk red dress. I watched him, as his eyes drank me in, lastly, landing on our baby bump.

He said nothing for a few moments. When he looked back up at me, he burst into tears. Immediately I went to

hug him, but instead, he buried his face into my lap. His arms wrapped around my waist, like it was his only life line and I knew, I had changed his mind.

I summoned up all of the beautiful things, I could think of. Him and I, running through the forest barefoot, as butterflies raced around us. I imagined what it would be like, to hold our newborn baby, and watch him grow. I felt the warm breeze of ocean air, and the sun hitting my face, to welcome me to a new day. The moon came up and we danced around a fire. Without even realizing it, I was humming a song. It was one, I didn't know consciously, but rather intuitively. I hummed, for as long as those beautiful thoughts came into my mind.

When they all stopped, I opened my eyes and saw a wide-eyed Dimitri, staring up at me, with no tears left to cry.

His eyes shone in wonder and amazement. There was no tragedy in them. A true transformation, just took place before me.

"Whoa." I breathed aloud.

"Whoa indeed." Atum somehow stood by the first pillar, mirroring the look I just saw on Dimitri.

Dimitri got up, and dropped his hand in a bow.

"Shall we?" he gestured.

"We shall," I replied in a cliche way, allowing him to help me up and guide me to the spot where Atum stood, watching the two of us.

"Return now. You have much more work to do, you two."

He smiled at the both of us, and then the world dissolved. I opened my eyes to a car full of people, staring at me, mouths open. I didn't feel a moving sensation, so I assumed we came to a stop.

I looked down and couldn't believe my eyes. Dimitri no longer looked like life was fleeing him. His skin held the same olive colour, one would after a day in the sunlight. His eyes were alert and alive. He smiled a radiant smile, then he sat up.

"Show me your back," I ordered, as I helped lift his shirt. The bullet holes were still there, but they looked more like bite marks. Blood was no longer flowing out of them. I ran my fingers over them, in pure astonishment.

I looked around, to see if my theory was correct, and sure enough, I found the bullets on the seat.

"What the hell happened?" Luca spoke first.

"He's healed." Victoria gasped.

"I can't believe it..." Myles spoke.

"Emilia.... how did you do that?" Sophia asked

"What does this mean?" Elizabeth said.

I simply couldn't answer any of these questions. I didn't know the answer to any of them, and I was exhausted.

"Is there anywhere near here, we can all go and be safe at?" Dimitri looked around the car. Everyone was so shocked, that they couldn't take their eyes off of us.

"A motel up north..." Myles mumbled out. He gave the coordinates to Luca, who could just barely grasp reality enough, to start ~~to~~ the engine and get us back on the main road.

"What are you thinking Dima?" I snuggled into him, despite his clothing being full of blood, and the seats covered with it.

"I'm thinking it's time for all of us to heal." He kissed my forehead and I faded into sleep.

14. The Baby

The aftermath of the rescue, was depressing. No one knew what to do, or what had even happened. Without Janica, Elizabeth, Victoria, and Sophia constantly blamed themselves, and were extremely sad to have lost her.

Luca became even more closed off without Donny, which was hard to do. Myles was suffering from extreme exhaustion. The entire mission was hard on someone, as old as he was. Dimitri felt the burden, of all the things, that could've been done, and held himself responsible, for everyone's sadness. And me? I was numb.

No one wanted to be away from each other, for fear the Anova's, would somehow find out everything that happened and come to find us. So, we all went to the place, we thought would be the safest: Athens.

After we arrived in Athens, we took the group to my parent's place, in the mountains. Some time had passed, before we decided, that no one was after us and we could return to everyday life.

Sophia and Victoria wanted to stay close to Dimitri and I, so we bought two houses next to each other, by the ocean. Myles and Elizabeth wanted to go back to Olympia, so they left together. Luca didn't know what he wanted to do, so he stayed with the two of us.

"Good morning, everyone," I joined the group for breakfast, at a beautiful spot, overlooking the sea. I had been running late – baby stuff – and joined them, right after the coffees had shown up.

"Good morning, Emilia. Here," Sophia handed me a cup, "I ordered an oat milk, london fog for you." I smiled and took the cup in return.

"Is everything okay?" Dimitri looked at me with concern, and slid his hand over my thigh.

"Yeah, fine. I'm just tired." I gave him a small kiss on the cheek and he relaxed.

I felt a twist of pain, in my heart, as I met Luca's eyes, from across the table. I was used to seeing Luca, ready for action. His black hair was short and always styled perfectly in a slicked back motion. His clothing was clean, all black and well put together. Those light blue eyes of his, attentive and observing.

However, today I barely recognized him. His hair was an absolute mess, and the length, suggested he hadn't gotten it cut, in a long time. For the first time ever, I saw facial hair on him. The sweat shirt and jeans, suggested he barely rolled out of bed, and his eyes? They were drowning with sorrow, contrasted by his deep bags, showing the lack of sleep he had been getting.

"Luca, how are you feeling?" I asked, extending my hand to reach is. I wanted to send him some healing.

He subtly moved away, just as we touched, "I'm fine."

Those were the only words he spoke, for the rest of ~~the~~ breakfast.

As for the rest of us, we exchanged light conversation.

No one dared, or wanted to talk about anything, to do with the Anova's. Sophia proposed, we all go to Vegas and start gambling.

205

"You still have to finish school, you know." Dimitri spoke in a big brother way, to her. Her cheeks flashed red, from embarrassment.

"Yes, you do." Victoria chimed in.

"Sophia, they're both right. School is important. It's been two months since you've gone." I told her in a stern voice, but every time, I looked into her deep brown eyes, I only felt deep love and admiration for her. She really had become my little sister.

"I know. I signed up to take courses, here in Athens. I had to pass an admission test," she held up a piece of paper, "and I did! I wanted to surprise everyone. That's why I asked you all, to go for a nice family breakfast." Her smiled showed so bright, I wondered why the sun even bothered to come out today.

"Congrats Sof!" Her mother grabbed her and hugged her tightly, in an embrace. I missed my own mom so much, but getting anywhere six months pregnant was a hassle.

Never mind, trekking up to a secluded mountain fortress. I looked over at Luca, who for the first time, since we arrived, was smiling at Sophia. He looked over at me and we locked eyes. Then his face went into shock.

"Emilia, your nose!" I frowned and touched my hand to it. I looked down and saw blood covering my hand.

Everyone threw napkins at me, so fast, I hardly had time to grab them.

"Are you okay?" Luca peered over me and inspected my entire face. He made it across the table, faster than lightening strikes the earth.

"Tilt your head forward my love, it'll help." I felt a warm hand against my lower back and recognized it as Dimitri's.

"Yes, I'm fine. Stop it." I put my hands up to defend myself.

"Okay, if you start feeling bad, you let me know okay?" Luca knelt down beside my chair, and put his hand on my thigh.

"Okay," I replied, with an annoyed expression. Then I realized, this man was the one suffering the most, so, I smiled warmly at him. He took the hint and returned to his chair.

Not much conversation happened after that. We wrapped up and headed home.

"I think, I need to go to the forest for a bit."

Dimitri and I stood in our new living room. It was bare, but we had the essentials.

"You can't go by yourself." Dimitri didn't want me going anywhere isolated, alone. There were a lot of factors. I was pregnant enough, that running away from a threat was difficult. Anova's could be anywhere, and we never knew what they looked like, until they made themselves clear. Plus, I think he was still hurt over the losses and mistakes. He wasn't wrong for these thoughts, but I didn't want to live in constant fear.

"I know you're paranoid, but I need this, like I need clean oxygen, Dima." I crossed my arms above my big belly.

"I'm not paranoid. I am protective. Those are two different things, Emilia. How are you supposed to let me know if something happens?" He stood in a posture that told me he was unhappy. Oh well.

"We have cell phones Dimitri. This isn't the beginning of time." I rolled my eyes at how stupid of a question that was.

I needed some alone time, in the forest. It was calling to me. I could feel it needed me too.

"Let her go, Dimitri." Luca spoke from the corner of the room, where he sat with his feet up on the table, throwing a tennis ball up in the air and catching it.

"Are you insane?"

"No. You know what she is capable of," he got up and came to stand in between us. "She brought you back from the dead, Dimitri. We watched you slowly die, in that SUV. You were dead. Then suddenly, you lit up. A bright light came from Emilia, and passed over to you. You both became this bright, shining light. It was so intense I had to pull over." We both looked at him confused. No one had brought up anything from the mission, other than a short memorial, we held for Donny and Janica.

"What else happened?" I asked, tapping his shoulder, so he would face me. He didn't move. He stood in front of me, like he was protecting me, from a wild animal. It was staggering, to see them face off like that. Dimitri was a few inches taller than Luca, but something in Luca's posture said that didn't matter... I didn't like the way this was going.

"Luca?" I spoke in a calm voice, while I touched his arm. I sent a little spirt into him. Immediately I felt more drained. What was that about?

He turned around with concern in his eyes, like he knew what I felt.

"What else happened that night, Luca?"

"We all saw you, bring him back to life. He died. Then he woke up. There's nothing else to say." He turned back around to Dimitri, "if you won't let her go alone, then offer to go with her. You're a big guy, you can handle what life throws at you."

Dimitri looked over at me, "is that okay with you? If I come along?"

I really didn't want anyone with me. I was having a lot of issues going on, and honestly, I was going out there to heal them. I had been to an Obstetrician and everything was fine with the baby, so I needed to go out there, to figure out what else could be wrong with me...

"Fine. But you have to wait in the car."

His only response was him staring at me.

"It's either you wait in the car, or you don't come."

"Fine."

"Fine, I'll go get ready." We ended up moving into a two-story house, with one bedroom on the main level, and an open concept upstairs. Because Luca was temporary, he slept up there on a pullout bed we bought. Dimitri and I's room, was on the main level. It was bare too, but very spacious, paired with large floor to ceiling windows. I went into the bathroom to clean up and change.

"Wow," I spoke aloud to myself, as I looked into the full-length mirror on the wall. My body had not only changed because of the baby, but because of the cuts I accumulated during our mission. I was full of post battle wound scars.

I looked at my tired self, and noticed the bags under my eyes. I sure didn't look twenty-two. Taking a deep breath, and a loud exhale, I decided not to dwell on my outer appearance. What I was, as a soul, was more important. I put a pair of leggings on, that fit, paired it with a long t-shirt and headed to the front door. I only saw Luca on the couch, as I walked out of the bedroom.

"Is he outside?" I asked as I went to grab my shoes.

"He's in the car."

"Then–" As I went to bend down, to grab my shoes, Luca was beside me.

"Let me help." He bent down and began to put my sneakers on for me. As he slipped my feet into my shoes, he was delicate and gentle. It caught me by surprise.

"Thank you," I managed to stumble out, as he stood to face me.

"You're welcome, Emilia. Be safe out there, God only knows what could happen," he reached out and played with a strand of my hair.

I grabbed his hand and held it to my face.

"Luca… I'm so sorry about Donny." Tears welled up, and spilled over my eyes. I hadn't had time, to talk to him about this yet, but it was weighing on me.

His expression mirrored mine in one of sorrow. His hand was still there, gently holding my face and wiping away my tears.

"I know," he whispered "me too."

I pulled him in, to as much of a hug as I could. The only distance between us was Dimitri and I's, baby.

I pulled away, and headed out to the car. Dimitri hopped out, and came to open my side. I slid into the passenger seat of his car, which was here in Athens, all along. He wasn't much of a car guy, but his family was extremely wealthy, and only wanted him to drive nice vehicles.

 They came to a compromise and bought him a black Porsche Panamera. If they had it their way, this would've been the most obnoxious Lamborghini in the world.

"Where to?" He asked as he slid into the seat, beside me.

I always wondered, how a man of his height and muscle size, could fit into such a small car, but he made it work gracefully.

"Take me to that waterfall, we love."

He pulled out of the driveway and I watched as Luca's face faded into the distance.

We drove to one of our favourite spots in Northern Athens. The fullness of the trees, reminded me of my home in Canada. To top it off, the waterfalls here, are a lot warmer. The ride from our new house, was about forty-five minutes. We made the trip in silence, which I didn't mind. Dimitri and I had been together, for such a long time, that the silence was just as enjoyable, as the conversations.

As we pulled up to park, I could sense something important was a happening in the trees.

"I will wait here, until you're done." He leaned over and kissed my forehead.

I didn't let him pull away. Instead, I grabbed the looseness of his shirt, and pulled him to me. I kissed him harder than I had in the last two months. The world, felt like a place that was constantly changing. I did love him so much. He pulled back, to break it off.

"Emilia… you need to go, remember?" He tilted my chin up, gently with his finger and smiled the most beautiful smile, I have ever seen on him. I sighed.

"You're right. I just love you so much Dima… You're hard to resist." With that, I turned and got out of the car.

I started to walk to a place we used to go, but a rabbit appeared. I decided to follow it and see where it would lead me.

I walked for a bit, and came to a perfect meadow. The grass was just under knee high, with a patch, I could tell deer had slept in. Along the edges of the meadow, wild flowers were in full bloom. The July weather was so beautiful in Greece, that all the birds were out chirping. I sat on the flat grass and laid back to look up at the clear blue sky. If there was one thing in this world I knew, it was the healing power of mother nature. Today wasn't the first day, I had a nose bleed. It had been happening for a while, just at times, when no one was around. I didn't want to admit to anyone, that I was having these, because I didn't want them to worry. I was a healer, how could I become sick?

A wolf came out of the woods, with deep amber eyes and I knew who it was.

"Hi," I spoke aloud, while trying to sit up. Being this pregnant, was such a drag.

Emilia, something is wrong.

"What's wrong?" I was puzzled.

With you, I can smell it.

"Can you smell what it is?" I asked.

Blood.

"Yeah, I've had like ten nose bleeds in the last week. I know something is wrong, that's why I'm here. To heal myself."

Maybe it isn't you, that needs to be healed.

The words stung me, as I tried to think what else, could be causing these nose bleeds. Everyone I knew, was reportedly okay, and the doctor said the baby was fine. The wolf and I stared at each other for a bit more, until I became tired again.

I felt weak, and knew I needed to get back to the car where Dimitri was, but I wasn't sure of the pathway. Using magic, was taking a lot out of me.

I pulled out my cell phone and immediately dialled Dimitri. I gave him the best directions as I could, then I laid back down again. I don't know how much time passed, but I kept fading in and out of consciousness. I would see the sky, then I would see black. I finally felt warm arms around me, and a beautiful scent of sandalwood, I would've recognized even if I were dead.

"Something...wrong," I mumbled, as I felt the movement of being carried.

"Emilia? Can you hear me? Emilia? We're almost at the car."

Mommy? Help me! Mommy? I heard this small female voice in my head. Who was it? Where was it coming from.

"Dima... stop" I managed to say.

"No." He kept walking.

Mommy? I'm sick, I need help!

"Dima... stop... please," I could feel the urge to throw up, coming on.

"We're almost there, Emilia." His voice was stern.

Mommy? Can you hear me?

"STOP!" I shouted. Dimitri listened and stopped, but didn't let me down.

"Down. Now." Was all I could say.

He let me down, but held me upright.

"What's wrong?" My head was spinning, and I didn't know how to reply. I held onto his arm, like it was the only thing in the world, that was keeping me upright.

Mommy?

I heard again, and just as the voice filled my mind, I threw up. Not just any throw up, but blood. Tons and tons of blood. Like any good fiancè, Dimitri panicked and held all my hair, far away from the mess.

After I was able to stop, I looked at the now painted red ground, and understanding began to set it. The blood represented a problem, going on inside of me. That voice wasn't the voice of an animal, or a fight outside, of me. That was the voice of my baby…a baby girl. I didn't ask the doctors the sex, because I was certain I knew. But that voice? I knew then and there.

It dawned on me, that I was having a daughter. And my daughter? She was in trouble. Something was very wrong.

I looked up at Dimitri, with so much fear in my face, that he instantly went pale.

"Are you okay?" He asked with a shaking voice, one I've never heard, on him before. He was less scared when he begged me to let him die.

"I don't know." I replied.

He took his shirt off, and helped me wipe the blood off of my face.

"It's a girl."

"What is?" He asked, puzzled. He was gentle with my skin, but his touch brought numbness to my heart. He tucked hair, behind my ears, as I looked straight into his chest, avoiding his eyes.

"The baby." I spoke.

"How do you know? " He asked, arching an eyebrow, while trying to soothe me.

"I heard her. She spoke to me." Tears started to roll down my cheeks uncontrollably.

"What did she say love?" He tilted my chin up, so that our eyes would meet.

"She's dying." I started to heavily, cry now.

Dimitri looked at me, looked at my belly and with one swift movement, lifted me up in his arms and carried me all the way to the car. He put the seat back, as far as he could, to mock a bed, and helped me feel comfortable.

He was silent, the entire time, and only spoke, when he got on the phone. The conversation took place, in Russian, a dialect I didn't fully comprehend.

"Who was that?" I asked barely able to keep my eyes open.

"Someone to help." His response was short, and his eyes never left the road.

"Will they meet us at our house?" My voice was trembling.

"No, we are going to them."

Epilogue: Russia

I woke up in a comfortable bed, staring at a wood ceiling, that looked like it could collapse at any moment.

"What the..." I managed to breath out, in absolute shock at my whereabouts.

"Emilia?" A warm, gentle touch I knew so well, grabbed a hold of my hand.

"Where are we?" I asked, still staring at the ceiling. I couldn't keep my eyes off it. I truly felt, if I looked away it would cave in.

"We're safe, Emilia. There is a woman here, Inge, who is has been taking care of you, since we arrived a few days ago."

"What!" I exclaimed, and I whipped my head over, to where he sat. As always, he took my breath away. The sudden look of his deep green eyes, took me away, from where I was. Suddenly, we were just floating there, together, bodiless. His eyes were my favourite place to get lost in.

I shook my head, regaining my awareness, "a few days, Dima? What happened?"

He let out a soft laugh, and leaned into me. His scent unwavering from sandalwood and juniper, "We flew here, a few days ago, you were in bad shape, and kept fading in, and out of consciousness. We got in a car, and drove out here to Igne's. She saw you, and immediately took you into care. This is the most stable, you've been since."

I sighed. I thought being reunited with Dimitri, would bring me a fairy tale ending. Instead, I ended up right back, at a cabin in the woods, running. Did time move forward, backwards, or not at all?

"So, what happens now?" I asked.

"We wait, and see." He touched my cheek, and I sank my face, right into his palm.

My safe place.

About the Author

Kai-Lee Worsley was born an only child into a single mother household. She grew up in and around poverty, shaping her to become the person she is today. Fiction novels were a way for Kai-Lee to escape the challenges she faced at home, and acted as a safe place for her to let her mind wonder. As a child, she enjoyed all things arts, music, and sports - particularly street hockey with the boys. In her child life, Kai-Lee wrote many short stories, sparking that inner knowing that she was always destined to be a storyteller. Warrior of Earth marks the first official publication for the young author with many more to come.

Manufactured by Amazon.ca
Bolton, ON